CLOSE ENCOUNTERS OF THE FIFTH KIND

The return of Roy Neary

By

Otis Record

According to Paranormal-Encylopedia.com:
The term *close encounter* was coined by American astronomer and ufologist **Josef Allen Hynek** (1910 - 1986) in his 1972 book *The UFO Experience: A Scientific Inquiry.*

Hynek proposed three types of close encounter:

First Kind: Sighting of one or more UFOs at a distance of 500 feet or less.

Second Kind: Sighting of a UFO with associated physical effects (e.g. heat, electrical interference, etc).

Third Kind: Sighting of an animated being (presumably an **alien** but not specifically defined as such.)

Since Hynek's original classification several more types have been suggested, although these are not universally recognized:

Fourth Kind: Human **abduction** by an alien. May also include voluntary experiences.

Fifth Kind: Voluntary bilateral contact between humans and extraterrestrials.

Acknowledgements

Thanks to God who gives the ability to imagine.

Thanks to my beautiful wife, Feonia, for putting up with all of the craziness over the years and for the encouragement to keep on writing.

Thanks to my sister, Joyce Powell, for the many hours of editing and moral support.

Thanks to my daughters, Melissa and Angela, and granddaughter, Angel, for encouragement and with editing for content and readability.

Thanks to my 11-year-old grandson, Chase, not for any particular reason other than just encouraging his old grandpa to keep writing.

The inspiration for this particular rendering came from my love of the movie Close Encounters of The Third Kind and the novel of the same name by Stephen Spielberg.

Cover by Otis Record.
Photo: visibleearth.nasa.gov

A note from the author

These are the questions that you have to ask yourself: Do U.F.O.s really exist or are the thousands of sightings each year just simply misidentified advanced military aircraft of our own making? Are the rumors of unidentified flying objects just a smoke screen to keep our newest weapons a secret from our many enemies? Is the military in league with an alien culture? If the military is in league with a highly advanced alien race, then why isn't their obviously superior technology impacting our lives? Are they holding out on us, selfishly refusing to share, or are they only giving us what they think we can handle? Are the aliens benevolent or are they calculating and dangerous? If they do exist, why isn't there any hard evidence? Is Homeplanet a planet at all or is it a construct created as a life boat for mankind?

In 1977, N.A.S.A. launched a deep space probe in a quest for data on (among other things) the mythical "Earth Two," long thought to be in a synchronous orbit on the opposite side of the Sun from "Terra Firma." They found nothing. Is it that we don't have empirical evidence for all of these questions or is it that we just don't remember?

In today's popular science fiction culture, many still remain hopeful that at least some of the disappearances are of extraterrestrial origin. We, as modern science fiction lovers (I think that I speak for the majority), would be all right with the adventure of going into space with interstellar Visitors as long as the real life abducted ones aren't being tortured or eaten, but, when it comes to fictional characters, frankly anything goes, right?

According to an article written for *Crime Library* (an internet based research site supplying crime statistics and other information) by David Krajick, in the United States alone it is estimated that approximately 2,300 people go missing every day. The emotional pain and suffering caused by these real disappearances is immense, and the author does in no means want to make light of the many horrific occurrences.

As in the case of the character Gus, the author describes an instance of mental illness giving symptoms that may seem to match some known mental diseases. It is not the intention of the author to denigrate any person known or unknown. Mental illness is no laughing matter.

It had been said that, although they had a horrible family life, Roy Neary's family deserved better than what they were given. Being a family man, I felt that Roy deserved a second chance, an opportunity to try and make things right for his family and for himself. This rendering is based in part on the family values put forth by Stephen Spielberg: "That was 1977. So I wrote that blithely. Today, I would never have the guy leaving his family and going on the mother ship".

There are many unknown forces from within and without that could destroy Roy's quest to return to Earth and to his family. Getting home is just a small part of his dilemma. He also has to consider the attitudes of the people that he desperately wants to reconcile with.

The story before you is about aliens, U.F.O.s, volcanic eruptions, airplane crashes, laser attacks, betrayal, murder attempts, mental breakdowns, abductions, rescues, and, let's not forget, cowboys, horses, hillbilly deer hunters, and rats.

This narrative is also about the human condition - obsession, abandonment, loss, anger, reconciliation, and vindication. Above all, it is about the glue that binds it all together - love, for ultimately true love conquers all.

Although the beginning premise is familiar this rendering was never intended to be a sequel, unofficial or official. It is just one possible scenario.

Prologue

In the beginning of the twentieth century, an illusory alien race of interstellar beings began visiting Earth. They would slip in and out of our solar system unnoticed for the most part. Occasionally, our best and brightest astronomers would catch a glimpse of them coming or going but before the ships could be differentiated from meteors, comets, asteroid fragments, etcetera, they would be out of frame and out of view. The reason being that the time it would take for the very best human technician to first realize that there was something unusual moving through the cosmos and then react by attempting to track the object long enough to snap a photo, the ship would be gone. Knowing this, the "Visitors" could come and go with impunity.

For some reason known only to them, they occasionally "borrowed" people and objects from around the world. The "borrowed" people came from all walks of life and time periods. One might be a young girl herding sheep on an Alpine meadow while another might be an Army pilot on maneuvers over the ocean. Sometimes people were abducted singularly and sometimes as many as 50 people at a time, as in one case concerning a commercial airliner. Sometimes people were abducted in a group as small as two or three. There seemed to not be any rhyme, reason, or pattern to these unexplainable abductions.

These people were sometimes, but not always, borrowed with equipment and objects that they were in contact with at the time, such as airplanes, boats, motorcycles, vehicles of all descriptions, and even one covered wagon.

In the latter part of the twentieth century, the extraterrestrials for some unknown reason decided to change their tactics. Instead of simply collecting individual specimens or groups of specimens and examining them, they decided to make direct contact with the human race. Through the implementation of a tonal vocabulary code (the use of various musical notes or tones designated to represent words, numbers, or letters of the alphabet), they made arrangements with "the powers that be" to return all of the borrowed ones that wished to return to Earth. Of the nearly two hundred humans onboard the "Mothership", most did. It was believed among Earth's analysts that the change in the "Visitor's" (also known as "little ones, tall ones, Friends, little Friends, Operators, Primary, Their, Them, and They") tactics came from understanding the emotional pain that they had thrust on their captives.

Knowing that the ties to their lives on Earth had long since died and finding the emotional trauma to be overwhelming, all of the returnees, of their own choice, had their memories wiped clean. With a new start and new identity, the returnees were free to build new lives, free from the dangers of being studied or manipulated. They were essentially just empty vessels retaining only the knowledge that they had prearranged to have. Out of the group there would be mathematicians, scientists, doctors, lawyers, artists, musicians, etcetera, achieving far above the levels they had aspired to in their former life. All of these new lives came with proper documentation, degrees, and guaranteed (you guessed it) government or military career paths. Although they were given great things, it was little payment for what was taken from them.

The site (Devils Tower Wyoming) was chosen jointly by the extraterrestrials and terrestrials for its remoteness and securability. The military establishment naturally insisted on stringent security measures but was quickly outvoted by the world-wide science community. The surprise to the whole reception committee would come in the form of several people from around the globe showing up on location, motivated by an implanted alien psychic vision, driving them to abandon their conventional lives. In that light, we come to the disappearance of our main character.

Roy was an ordinary young man by anyone's account. He had a wife (Ronnie), three children, (Bradford "Brad" age 8, Tobias "Toby" age 6, and Sylvia "Sylvie" age 4) that he adored, a house with a sizable mortgage, and a fairly new car that he was about to pay off. So what was there about Roy that drew the attention of the extraterrestrials or, for that matter, the others that had been taken in the past? Roy, was one of the only two (the other being Jillian, Barry's mother) to successfully reach the Visitor's landing site at Devil's Tower. The rest were forced from the area by the military. Roy had previously met Jillian and Barry while pursuing one of the small ships, nearly running Barry down on the road in the process. Barry had run away from home in search of his "little friends," with Jillian hot on his trail, when he popped out on the road in front of Roy's speeding truck. The close call and Roy's apologetic attitude caused Jillian and him to become friends.

In preparation for the "Visitation," there had been a team of explorers meticulously chosen and trained by the science and military communities for the trip off planet, but, despite the best laid plans of the Earthlings, the extraterrestrials chose Roy in the place of one of their bravest and brightest, the actual chosen leader of the interstellar excursion. During the prisoner exchange (the borrowed ones didn't go of their own free will), Barry (then 5 years old), who had been abducted (the only good term for the situation because he was a child despite the fact that he wanted to go with them), was returned to his mother, Jillian. The main difference between Roy and the rest laid in the fact that he was the only one of the civilians that went with Them of his own free will. Even though Roy was drawn to the site by a tormenting psychic vision, ultimately it was his decision to abandon his family and go with Them. Jillian, on the other hand, was drawn to the site not only by the vision but, more importantly, by the need to find her son Barry, which was quite possibly the only reason that she was invited.

Chapter 1
Obsession

Southern California

Roy Neary was dead, or at least most of his family thought so. Some held out a glimmer of hope but, for at least one, the hurt and anger was too overwhelming.

"Good riddance to a man that deserted his family, no matter what the reason."

Going with the aliens and exploring the cosmos for over thirty Earth years was a decision that Roy deeply regretted.

"If I had known that we would be gone so long, I would have said no."

***

"Roy! Roy! Where are you?"

"I don't know, Mom!"

Ronnie Smith, a thin, frail, hospital-bound, terminally ill woman in her sixties, for the last couple of days had been asking for her long lost husband, Roy - the husband that had left her with three young children to bring up on her own; the husband that had disappeared 30 some odd years before after having an apparent psychotic break from reality.

What had caused the young family man to suddenly slip away from a normal ordinary life in the suburbs? What could have possibly pried him away from apparent sanity? These were the questions on everyone's mind, well, everyone in the tight-knit circle named Smith that is.

The night that the shadows of mental distress began to creep into their lives was the night that there had been a power outage in a large section of their county. But there had been power outages before! Why would this particular one push him over the edge? What had happened out there in the darkness?

Roy had been a lineman for the local electric cooperative for almost ten years, since his graduation from state college with an electrical engineering degree. He had not even so much as gone in late or called in sick until the night the nightmare began.

Roy was a fun loving wild man in his late twenties, who frequently pulled outrageous pranks on his family and friends and was more than willing to receive as good as he gave. Like many humans, Roy was a complex soul having the normal ebb and flow of emotions, but he had never, even remotely, been considered to be disturbed.

There had been no warning signs, no tell tale ramblings or changes of personality. It was as if he just inexplicably emotionally imploded. It was like some sort of reality switch had been flipped to the neutral position!

Alarmingly and without warning for the next two nights, he had ran outside like a man possessed by someone or something, unashamedly standing in their back yard or on the roof of their house, staring at the night sky, and yelling, "What is it? What is it?"

Soon after Roy that had begun running around the house in broad daylight, covered in mud, his hair a total mess, a frightened look on his face, franticly throwing dirt, rocks, and shrubbery into the house through a couple of broken windows. The young father had been ranting and raving like a wild man and, at times, laughing out loud, while yelling, "I know this! I know this!" Although he didn't know it at the time, he was building a replica of the aliens landing zone. Shortly afterward, Ronnie, Roy's wife of a little over ten years, had taken their children and moved in with her mother on the other side of the state. She had thought at the time that it was the right thing to do. After all, someone had to be the sane one.

The neighbors almost immediately became afraid to go outside, limiting their activities to skulking from window to window, peeping through gaps in their curtains. In that day and time, everyone tried to mind their own business, but the consensus of the neighborhood gossips was to call the police even though Roy hadn't shown any dangerous or violent actions toward anyone but himself. But before they could, he realized what he had actually been building. Driven nearly insane by the psychic attack, Roy rented a car (Ronnie had taken the family car) and just disappeared!!!

Fearing that Roy was mentally compromised and possibly a danger to himself or others and finding evidence that he had left the state, the local sheriff had turned the case over to "higher powers." The F.B.I. then tracked him as far as Wyoming through credit card receipts. Within days they found his rental car, nearly destroyed and strangely abandoned in an area near Devils Tower, cordoned off by the military due to a freight train derailment. A train that was reported (actually a ruse cleverly constructed by the military) to be transporting, among other things, an unmarked, unregistered tanker filled with deadly weapons-grade nerve gas. The National Guard searched diligently for him for several weeks during and after the spill had been cleared, but they found no trace. He was gone, just gone! It seemed that he had completely vanished off the face of the Earth.

***

Brad, now nearly forty years old, the eldest of Roy and Ronnie's three children, stood at his mother's bedside absorbed in thought. His father had disappeared over 30 years ago. Why was she asking for him now? She had hardly mentioned him or their short life together in all of those years - not since changing their last name and moving to California, that is.

It had been hard all these years not having a real father around, and the anger and hurt was so deep that the little family had tried to wash him completely out of their minds. Even so, nagging questions lingered: Where? How? Why? Living in the past was something the whole family tried to avoid. What was done was done. Too much time had passed to do anything about it anyway. It was well known among the three Smith children, Brad, Toby, and Sylvia, that it was a closed subject and always would be.

There had been no reason to be angry about his father's lack of support or protection. The lifestyle and security the small family enjoyed, sadly, was far better than he could have provided anyway. The great loss was the love that could have been. To be honest, at least for Brad, it was good riddance to a man that had deserted his family no matter what the reason.

Brad pushed the call button hanging from his mother's bed.

"May I help you?"

"Yes, my mother needs your help!"

"I'll be right there!"

Ronnie was still tossing and turning when a trio of nurses arrived in her room. The squeak of the nurse's shoes on the highly polished floor, the rustle of the freshly starched uniforms, and the caring lilt of their voices always had a calming effect, a tiny bit of reassurance in the midst of the storm. The eldest of the three women, Head Nurse Lake, a classically beautiful, pleasingly plump, average height lady of Nordic descent, her graying hair tucked up tight under her nurse's hat and stethoscope hanging around her neck, stepped up close to the side of the hospital bed and gently took Ronnie's hand.

The youngest of the other two nurses, Nurse Wilks, a tall, very thin, African-American woman who was usually very upbeat and chatty, and Nurse Adams, a petite freckle-faced red-haired young woman with a wicked sense of humor, silently took up positions at a computer console located on a desk across from the foot of the bed and immediately began checking Ronnie's medical records.

"What's wrong, sweetie? What can I do for you?"

Ronnie was curled up in the fetal position on her specially ordered, overstuffed, hospital bed that was more like a huge pillow than a bed. (a special acquisition in appreciation for Ronnie's volunteer work and past donations totaling almost $1,000,000), or at least that was what the hospital staff was told. She continued mumbling something too faint for Brad and Head Nurse Lake to make out and then rolled over on her other side with her back to the door.

"She seems to be incoherent and getting more agitated by the minute, nurse."

The nurses busied themselves checking Ronnie's vital signs and trying to comfort their dying patient. Then, Head Nurse Lake stepped back from Ronnie's bedside and spoke quietly with Nurses Wilks and Adams. After a short discussion, Nurse Wilks silently left the dimly lit room to call the attending doctor. When the young nurse returned, Ronnie was given a mild sedative, injected into the drip line taped to her arm. Head Nurse Lake turned to Brad and spoke in hushed tones.

"This should help her to rest. The doctor said that it would be too dangerous to let her heart rate get out of control. Do you know what upset her?"

"I have no clue. She started waking up like usual and the more conscious she became, the more agitated she became. What little that I could make out made no sense. Do you think she is slipping into dementia?"

"Anything is possible with the medication keeping her blood pressure so low, but there hadn't been any signs of it before. I think she was just having a bad dream. Sometimes toward the end reality becomes a little blurred."

***

Ronnie's mind was still racing. She was positive that the voice she had heard was her long lost husband's. But how could that be? He had been gone so long, and, for all she knew, he was dead. The voice, sometimes clear and sometimes muddled, had been slipping into her dreams for the last several nights, but now she had been hearing "Him" when she was awake. Ronnie was beginning to wonder if her son Brad was right. Maybe she really was losing her grip on reality. As the sedative began coursing through her veins, Ronnie began to relax, causing the voice in her head and the voices in the room to quickly become distant. Ronnie drifted back off to sleep, peacefully floating in a drug-induced euphoria.

***

Somewhere in the Cosmos

The choking red dust rising from the trucks in the front of the caravan caused the visibility to diminish to near zero and the tension among the small group of student adventure seekers was almost unbearable. Earlier that morning part of the group had inexplicably decided to go ahead on their own against all logic and advice from their tour guides. Their excitement was to be expected. After all it was their first trip to Africa. Somehow one of the native guides was talked, or most likely bribed, into taking them out before dawn to observe a watering hole. The safari outfitter had not heard from them for hours, and now the main group was anxiously searching for them.

The temperature was already over a hundred degrees and it wasn't even noon yet, but the prospect of seeing totally wild and free exotic animals up close made the danger and discomfort worth it. After an hour of low gear creeping through dry washouts and savanna brush, the caravan emerged onto the open African plain. After several more minutes, the vehicles finally picked up speed. The lead vehicle was cresting a small hill when the driver suddenly slammed on the brakes, causing the small caravan of trucks to slide to a stop. Obscured by the billowing dust, the back three vehicles nearly collided with the ones in front of them. Supply boxes, duffle bags, and one unfortunate native guide went tumbling off the top of the outfitter's lorry that was bringing up the rear.

Directly in front of the lead truck sat the missing land rover, empty, canvas doors ripped off, with its engine still running. Beyond that lay the motorcycle that one of the guides had rode off on earlier that morning. The scene was simply horrifying. Blood was everywhere but no bodies. At first, their minds couldn't comprehend what could have possibly occurred there. The dazed group started to get out of their vehicles when they were quickly surrounded by a ravenous pride of lions, already blood-covered by the previous kill. Seeking refuge in their vehicles, the horrified tourists huddled together awaiting the first wave of attacks. The lions roared viciously as they circled their intended victims, growing bolder by the second, driven by hunger and blood lust. One of the native guides raised his rifle, shooting and killing one of the ten lionesses that were obviously starting an attack run.

Easily leaping up onto the hood of one of the land rovers, the bigger of the two male lions in the pride began ripping his way through the canvas top of the lead truck to reach the terrified occupants inside. When all seemed lost, a very loud annoying sound began echoing across the savanna. The sound appeared to be emanating from one of the trucks and sounded like someone was using a jackhammer on the side of a church bell.

Roy was trying to catch his breath as he reached for the snooze button on his old windup, double bell alarm clock.

"Wow, what a crazy dream!"

Sweaty and shaking, he quickly shook off the psychological angst caused by the deeply disturbing dream and gathered his thoughts. Roy wondered to himself what this day would hold. Would he be emotionally torn apart by the family he had abandoned those many years ago like an ill-fated safari on the plains of Africa?

Abandoned, that was a very harsh description of what happened all those years ago, but Roy had come to grips with the fact that it was exactly what he had done. No excuses, it had been his choice despite the circumstances leading up to his departure from Earth. Roy didn't know how his family would react to his delayed return, but he did know one thing. This would be a day for the record books.

Rubbing the sleep from his blue-gray eyes, Roy looked around the small apartment that he had called home for the last 30 years. He was comforted by the familiar, as most humans are. That is why he hadn't changed much in the room for several years. Roy had decorated his abode in the style that he was most familiar with. He called it early chaos, but his friends, human and non-human, just called it a mess.

There was a single-sized bed along one wall with a goose down pillow and a patchwork quilt, just like the one he remembered from his childhood. Roy had placed a small nightstand next to the head of the bed with an unremarkable lamp and the windup, double bell, alarm clock that he broke at least once a week. In the bookshelf headboard, there were piled several very worn-looking books of varying descriptions and an electronic reader pad with the monitor still lit up from the night before. Although he had unlimited access to the knowledge of the universe, Roy still immensely enjoyed the feel of the paper and allure of the familiar. He drew comfort from the tactile connection with something from his Earth life, even though he now had most of the volumes on board memorized. The library, although varied, was limited to a couple of hundred books and magazines borrowed from the airplanes and ships that had been returned to Earth during what Roy called the first "Visitation." He knew that the Visitors ships had been to Earth several times over the last century or two, as evidenced by the odd collection of people and things that had been returned, but 30 years ago was the first time that the contact had been official. Roy believed it was because Earth had advanced enough technologically and psychologically to be able to handle the truth: **WE ARE NOT ALONE**.

The walls of his tiny apartment were painted red with white stripes today, which made Roy chuckle because the colors clashed with the purple shag carpet that had appeared the day before. The interior of the room, or for that matter the entire ship, had no particular color scheme other than what was chosen by the "Operators." The Operators, as Roy called them, could choose any color, shade, or pattern at will for the interior or exterior of the ship. He didn't know if it helped alleviate the doldrums of space for the non-human population but it certainly did for the human population, and everyone including the guest humans took turns in the decision-making process. Although there were infinite sights to see while probing the depths of the known and unknown universe, there were also great gaps between galaxies and universes. The emptiness of the great expanse could close in on the unprepared mind. The term space, given for these gaps by

Earthlings, was simply and descriptively accurate. Roy wasn't sure if the color schemes in his room were an attempt at humor by the Operators or if they just had a poor sense of style.

He always looked forward to waking up from his sleep cycle because, not only were the wall and floor colors different every time, the photos were always different too. On the walls were hundreds of three-dimensional photographs. Although he felt comfort from the familiar, he also felt no small amount of peace from the constant changes in the information that he received from home.

It had been a long time since Roy had been with his family in their little home in Indiana and although he, from the beginning, had received daily updates on their well being, including surveillance photos, it was not like being there personally.

After 30 years, Roy still didn't fully understand the communication technology that was available, but he is very thankful for it. All he knew for sure is that data, such as audio and video, could be transmitted at millions of times the speed of light, bouncing from planet to planet through the use of "re-transmitter" units that not only boost the signal speeding it back up from jump to jump, but also keeping the signal one hundred percent intact. He learned from his little mentors that the re-transmitters were secretly being placed on all of the billions of planets by the "Master builders."

The Master builders, all of which, as far as Roy could tell, were still alive on the home planet and were not super intelligent as one would suppose. According to the little information that he had gathered on them, the mysterious Master builders had a lifespan many times longer than their human counterparts. But who knew what was normal or natural about them? According to his limited sources, the

Master builders were only able to create all of the wonderful technology simply because they had the time to complete their thought processes over the span of hundreds, perhaps thousands, of years.

To explain their process of expanded design and invention simply, if your life cycle was extended to even four hundred years and if you were a farmer tilling the ground with a rock tied to a stick, would you continue doing it the same way for hundreds of years or would you think of a better way?

Roy had not aged during his time away from Earth and none of the other humans had either. This hadn't been possible before the Master builder's discovery of the life lengthening medical procedures employed on Homeplanet and on each of their ships. When Roy asked them about the knowledge that they had about human physiology, he was told that everything they knew was given to them. His very limited sources among Operators didn't offer any more of an explanation than that, and Roy figured that, if they wanted him to know more, they would tell him. The mystery of the Master builders was perplexing to Roy because the little he did know about his alien Friends was that they didn't age or die. As far as he could tell, they didn't procreate either. Secretly he suspected that the Master builders might be a completely different species than his little grey Friends. As far as he could figure out, the Master builders might have even built them. In the years of travel on one Mothership and then another, he had never met even one of the ancient engineers.

Roy slid his medium build, 5'10" body out of bed, tossing the quilt aside. He sat up, digging his toes into the thick pile of the purple shag carpet. Roy chuckled again about the colors in the room. He stretched and yawned before stumbling toward the shower that had begun running at the perfect temperature the second his feet hit the floor. The bathroom was once again modeled after the familiar, with all of the usual appliances and accoutrements. Roy wiped the steam from the mirror and saw an image of the old man he should have become during his years with the Visitors. The thin grey hair, the wrinkled brow, and the droopy eyelids were a reminder of how fortunate he was to be "chosen." He laughed out loud at his image, knowing that the "Operators' were having a little fun at his expense. The mirror blinked, revealing Roy's true present image. Thanks to their medical expertise, especially concerning the human ageing process, he actually at that time, looked and felt like a twenty-something. Although it was meant to be an attempt at humor, Roy was overtaken by a wave of melancholy caused by the fact that his beloved Ronnie, now in her late fifties, didn't have access to this technology and was dying because of it. Roy combed his curly black hair and brushed his nearly perfect teeth. He smiled at his reflection and thought, "I'm glad Sylvie got Ronnie's good looks." Roy was very proud of all of his children, but his little blond baby girl held a special place in his heart. It was hard to admit to himself that she was a grown woman. Even in her thirties, she was still as cute as a button, a near carbon copy of her mother - 5'6", slender, radiant blond hair, and a smile that could warm the coldest heart; the only difference was that Ronnie had hazel eyes and Sylvia had blue eyes like Roy. Sylvia even had Ronnie's wicked sense of humor and mental tenacity. Roy was really looking forward to getting to know his family again, if they would let him that is.

***

The Visitors thought it was very amusing that the humans aboard the ship did the things that they did, even though they really didn't have to. Although Roy and the other humans had explained to their hosts that the daily bodily functions and maintenance was what kept them feeling human, it was still hard for them to understand. The concept of having to breathe air, eat, sleep, bathe, exercise, etcetera, etcetera, to maintain emotional balance was hard to grasp for a race of beings that were sustained by silicon nutrients derived from cosmic dust and the energy of the universe itself.

After showering and shaving, Roy took several minutes perusing the updated photos. He was becoming more and more concerned over his wife Ronnie's medical condition. To see her lying there in a hospital bed wasting away was causing his heart to break. Hopefully, it would be all over soon, but he knew as well as anyone that death can't be predicted accurately or definitively stopped. Oh sure, the little interstellar beings had the technology to repair organs and bodily systems and by doing so life could be extended greatly, but if it is your time to go, it's your time to go. After all, there has been only one that conquered death and lived to tell about it.

Roy concentrated on pushing the sadness and anxiety aside because today he was a happy man, because today he was going home. That is if you could call it a day. The sleep cycles were needed to keep one's physical and psychological equilibrium in check, but they didn't coincide with daylight and dark as on Earth. It took a lot of getting used to, but after awhile everything seemed natural.

After a quick full body blow dry (one of the many conveniences that didn't fit the theme of the apartment), Roy put on his all-purpose jump suit and running shoes and once again snickered about the choice of room colors. Stepping out the door of his little apartment, he once again stood in awe of his surroundings. After three Earth decades onboard the immense star cruisers, he was still amazed.

A garden was directly in front of him, actually more like a jungle, that contained nearly every species of plant known to these ancient space explorers, all of the non-poisonous ones that is. Roy yawned, stretched, and took a deep breath. The air was cool and clean, as after a spring rain. Water droplets were falling from the lush canopy overhead just the way he liked it. Roy squinted at the artificial sunlight filtering down through the leafy vines and branches overhead. The fragrance of a myriad of exotic blossoms wafted through the garden, carried on an artificial breeze. It was almost as if the sun was really shining on some primordial rain forest at the dawn of time. Everything about this section of the ship was exactly the way Roy liked it the most and was all by design. He was about to embark on a difficult time in his life, and his little Friends were apparently trying to make it as easy as possible.

Taking one of the shorter paths this morning, Roy wanted to work off some anxiety without tiring out too much. If one desired, there were paths that were quite taxing and required great skill to traverse. There were hills and cliffs to climb, waterfalls and creeks to ford, and grotto pools to swim in. One could spend days exploring if they so desired. On the eventuality that the human mind would become bored with the familiar, the whole garden matrix could be rearranged with a thought and a wave of what passed for a hand. Although he missed his life on Earth, Roy had to admit that he really did love the life he had come to know. The only thing missing was the people he loved most.

Roy enjoyed the solitude of his morning run, it was nearly three miles from one end of the garden to the other on the short trail, and he knew he wouldn't see anyone else along the way, unless he was in the mood for company. There were over 800,000 souls on board the ship, including 20 other humans, and he knew everyone by name. Well, the term "name" was a weak description because the nonhumans on board didn't really communicate verbally. They made a sort of chirping sound when they were excited about one thing or another, but the real communication between themselves and others was all done telepathically. Roy couldn't explain it himself, it was more like a feeling of intimate spirit knowledge instead of a passing acknowledgment of personality and physical attributes. There was no one that he just vaguely remembered. Among the multitude aboard, there wasn't a stranger among them.

It wouldn't seem possible but everyone on the ship could have as much privacy and as much togetherness as they desired. The nonhumans could speak to each other telepathically one at a time or to any combination of beings at the same time, but they considered it rude to look into another's thoughts or to force communication of any kind without permission, unless it was an emergency. That alone was the reason for giving Earth a tonal vocabulary on the first Visitation. These kind and gentle beings just didn't want to overwhelm and terrify the population. The act of openly showing themselves had been an intrusive, but necessary, move if the great design of the Master builders was ever to come to fruition. Their ultimate goal was the unifying of all sentient beings throughout the known and unknown universes beyond, eventually culminating in a peaceful society of interstellar Friends. The invitation would not be based on intelligence but rather on the ability to achieve and maintain self control. Roy wasn't sure where he exactly fit into their plans, but, other than being away from his family, he was very happy to be with them.

One of Roy's favorite spots overhung the cavernous central chamber of the ship and ran nearly sixteen miles around the internal circumference of the ship. The expansive mezzanine included the garden, a huge communal gathering area large enough to hold a major league baseball stadium, and enough open area to store as many "borrowed" objects as needed.

The little one's living quarters, if one could call them living quarters, were in perfect geometric order around the interior surface of the mammoth sphere, giving each and every one of the ship's occupants an unobstructed view of the interior of the ship. Each cubical, including the humans' quarters (which were much bigger), had an oval viewer panel on the outer wall that functioned as a porthole of sorts to space. The little ones quarters consisted of little more than what Roy surmised to be a sleeping pod (although they didn't sleep) and a monitor that seemed to hang in the air like some sort of holographic projection. The interior sides of their quarters were completely open to full view. Only the humans had provision for privacy. Although the Friends didn't understand, they accepted it as just another aspect of being human.

Roy had often observed his little Friends communicating. Were they operating the ship? Were they talking to Friends on the ship? Were they communicating with family on Homeworld? Do they have family as we think of family? These were some of the questions that Roy found to be too rude to ask. He was well aware that these amazing little creatures were dynamically telepathic, but to see them silently staring at one another in the monitors always made him chuckle. It must have been a human thing, because Roy found the whole process to be intriguing and oddly funny. It did make him acutely aware that what he did know about this alien society was miniscule, compared to what he didn't know.

There was no need for walkways or corridors between the floors and sections of the ship. The artificial gravity field didn't extend past the edge of the observation platform that lay directly in front of each of the domicile cubicles. All one would have to do, when a person desired to go to a work station or visit the many communal areas on the ship, would be to simply leap from your front porch into the weightless zone of the central area. Sometimes there were no leapers in the central chamber and sometimes there were thousands. There seemed to be no rhyme or reason for these peculiar migrations. It was too hard for Roy to figure out so he gave up trying. One thing that he did realize one day was that the Operators had produced an invisible air bubble that somehow surrounded the human passengers at all times, allowing them to enjoy all parts of the ship, including the gravity-free central chamber. Roy literally stumbled upon the knowledge when he accidently tripped over his own feet and fell off of the mezzanine. He didn't think that it was very funny at the time, but the Operators found it to be hilarious.

From his favorite vantage point on the mezzanine, Roy could watch the comings and goings of the planetary survey crews, diplomatic excursions, and sometimes what appeared to be just plain joy riding trips. The pure joy that these beings exhibited in their lives and especially in their flying was phenomenal. Roy didn't believe that they knew how to fly a straight line. Sometimes the small ships would race around and around inside of the ship just for fun. He had come to the conclusion that the ship was hollow simply to allow for flights of fancy. Everything that the little beings did was with excitement and gusto. Roy felt that, although they possessed an intellect of extraordinary degrees, they also possessed the heart and innocence of a young child.

As Roy came to the end of his morning run, he could see a small mixed group of individuals standing at the edge of the immense communal mezzanine. The group was comprised of three of Roy's little Friends, one Tall One, and a human female

(Roy considered her a friend of the human kind). The normal physical condition of the Friends was the seemingly fragile frame of the little ones. Standing about three feet tall, pale gray to slightly silver in color with large pupil-less black eyes, they all looked identical to Roy, it was just one more thing that he couldn't figure out and wouldn't ask about. The saying, "They all look alike to me," didn't apply because they really did all look alike. Thinking back over the years and his dealings with the aliens, Roy couldn't remember ever seeing any that appeared to be a child or with child. The Tall Ones on the other hand, were comprised of a small group of ancient explorers that had been caught in deep space, far from Homeplanet, without gravitational control. They stood seven to eight feet tall and were a stretched out version of the Little Ones. The effects of deep space had caused the irreversible condition of elongation, making them look like stick figures. Roy still didn't understand much about his host's physical attributes but found their abilities to stretch at will like silly putty to be simply amazing.

The group of Friends and the human female friend stood silently while watching the ship's progress towards Earth through a movie screen sized transparent portal in the side of the ship, a window into space, as it were. They all knew that this Visitation would be far different than the last one. There would be no need for any of the small ships to make an open appearance, no tonal vocabulary, no abductions, and no implanted psychic visions. The essential contacts had already been made. Earth's governments had been in constant contact with the Mothership and Homeplanet ever since they were allowed to interface with the secret re-transmitter buried deep inside Devil's Tower. This time the Mothership was there, after traveling hundreds of thousands of light years, for one purpose and only one purpose, to bring Roy home.

"What's up, guys?"

"Good morning, Roy. Did you have a restful sleep cycle?"

There were similar cheerful mental greetings from everyone in the group except one, the human female.

"We're almost to your drop off spot behind Jupiter, Roy! Where have you been? Did you break your alarm clock again?"

"No, Mary. I just couldn't stand to pace up and down the concourse all night so I put on the sleep wave module and got some sleep. I knew it was going to be an exhausting couple of days, and I would need all the rest that I could get. Hey! Just because you are a lot older than me doesn't make you my mother!"

"Very funny! Ha! Ha! Someone needs to keep you in line!"

"I know. That's why you love me."

"Yes, sir, you're like the son I never wanted."

"Yes Mom."

"You are giving up way too easy. Are you alright?"

"Sorry, Mary, I have a lot on my mind."

"What's going on Roy? Is something wrong? Aren't you going to get your family?"

"Well, Ronnie should be here with me soon, I hope. She is very sick, nearing the point of death, and they don't have the medical technology that she needs on Earth. I hope we get there in time."

"I'm so sorry, Roy. I knew she was sick, but I had no idea that her illness had progressed to that degree."

"We started toward Earth as soon as we knew that there was a problem. Medicine on your world is still inaccurate and nearly barbaric."

"I should have told you, Mary. Remember, us humans are often stubborn and keep things to themselves, sometimes very important things. I am very happy that the ship was able to alter course and bring me home five Earth years early."

"It had to be so."

"Do you think she will agree to come with us, Roy?"

"I hope so. I won't know how angry and hurt she really is until I actually see her. She may not even want to see me. I can't tell from the reports if the "Whispering" is going to help or hinder with the situation.

"Whispering? How are you whispering to her?"

"Well, because she is so critical, the Controllers and I felt that just showing up at her bedside might kill her. So, with their help, I have been very subtly implanting vague concepts and foggy ideas into her mind telepathically and trying to rekindle the love that we once shared. Actually, I have been whispering to them all."

"Them all?"

"My kids."

Mary was taken aback by Roy's explanation. She had never thought of him as being that deep or that romantic. All she could do was stand there with a puppy dog look on her face. Roy chuckled to himself. He had never known Mary to be speechless.

"I am approaching it very carefully. All that I can tell you right now is that she was getting agitated by it so I stopped. I don't know what kind of affect it is having on the kids."

"What will you do if she and your kids won't see you?"

"I plan on staying for the rest of my life if need be and trying to convince them otherwise. I have arranged for Ronnie to be regenerated whether she agrees to come or not. It is the least I can do after what I have done to her."

Mary was quiet to the point that the conversation had become one sided and awkward for both of them. She was beginning to look like she might burst into tears.

"Or I could do this."

Roy grinned, stepped toward the edge of the communal mezzanine, and then hopped outward, doing a back flip into the cavernous interior of the ship.

"I hate you Roy!!! I hope the rest of your family isn't crazy like you!!!!"

"They are, but you are going to love them!!!"

Roy plummeted several miles toward the floor of the ship until he was clear of the artificial gravity field and then gently floated to about twenty feet above the deck.

"I should leave you out there for a while Roy. It would serve you right."

"You love it, and you know it."

"Yes, but I sometimes wonder why your human companions haven't pushed you out a space lock yet. Don't think I haven't considered it myself."

"You wouldn't, and you know it. You would miss me too much. Besides, it's your fault that I am here. All I did was answer your call."

"We thought it was a good idea at the time."

"Having second thoughts are we?"

The little being didn't respond telepathically, It simply exhibited a huge smile (an action he had learned from the human population) and then chirped several times.

The city-sized Mothership dropped out of light speed and made preparations to come a stop on the dark side of Jupiter. This Mothership was a mega class star cruiser and much larger than the one that entered Earth's atmosphere during the last Visitation nearly 30 years earlier. Being nearly five miles in diameter and spherically shaped, it was too hard to hide from prying eyes if it got too close to an unsuspecting planet's population. The return route had been meticulously planned making sure to keep a very large planet (in this case they had chosen the largest planet in Earth's solar system, Jupiter) between the approaching interstellar ship and Earth.

"We are coming to a stop behind the planet you call Jupiter. It is time for you to board your shuttle. Good luck with your family, Roy. I mean that."

"Good luck. How extraordinary. I didn't think you believed in luck. Thank you very much old friend. I will need it."

The Operator began chirping again at the sight of Roy flailing around in an attempt to get moving.

"Would you like some assistance?"

Roy was a very confident man, but he did know when to ask for help.

"Thank you very much. That would be great."

"You are welcome."

With that, the Operator reconfigured the gravity bubble around Roy, lowering him to the floor, and making it possible for him to quickly bound several yards at a time toward the awaiting saucer-shaped shuttle that was resting on what could loosely be called a hanger deck. The saucer was one of a kind, designed by Roy in his spare time. He liked the look of the flying machine, and his hosts found it to be amusing. The actual shape of the shuttle ships really didn't matter. Their onboard repressor field generators created force field bubbles, giving anything inside that bubble a super slippery movement path in any direction, at nearly any speed. The bubble would simply push space, atmosphere or anything else out of the way on a sub-molecular level then reassemble it on the other side. Only living beings and animals could be harmed by the process so the ships were designed to avoid or evade anything that could be harmed.

No matter what the shape or size of the ship, there was no friction to deal with. It took very little energy to actually move the object inside the bubble. Combining the Repressor Field with a Bymagnetis Stabilizer and the effects of acceleration, deceleration, torque, and gravity had no effect on the inside or outside of the bubble. Motion was created by squeezing the molecules at the opposite end of the bubble from the desired direction making it possible to make instant starts, stops, and ninety degree turns that seem impossible to Earth observers. A ship with these capabilities wouldn't even ruffle a cloud or make a sonic boom. They were absolutely silent and impervious to detection and damage. All of the effects demonstrated during the first Visitation were for one purpose, to get the attention of Earth's governments.

***

Somewhere on a highway in Nebraska

The temporary landing strip was eerily silent considering the extraordinary events of the last few hours. The energy wave of the antigravity force generator was making everyone's skin tingle as the huge interstellar ship hovered silently just feet above the tarmac. Just seconds before, a huge ramp had descended from its brightly illuminated interior. Now, standing directly in front of the line of trained "Astronauts" was an alien being. This was not a chance meeting. It was the conclusion and beginning of many years of work. An agreement of sorts had somehow been reached with these interstellar beings, an accord that was exciting beyond belief and just as terrifying.

The moment had come. The young intelligence officer stood silently awaiting his turn. A small oval eyed being had half walked, half floated toward his position in the line of candidates. He was expecting full well to be ushered up the ramp and into the awaiting spacecraft with the other "astronauts". His extreme disappointment quickly turned to frustration and then to anger as all but one of the trained operatives were chosen. To make matters worse, the one that the aliens chose wasn't even one of the government approved team, but a stranger.

How could they reject him? How could they choose that civilian? Where did that interloper come from anyway? These questions only enraged him more, but he stood there silently seething, controlling the urge to strike out vocally, if not physically.

Suddenly, one of the little creatures was back at his position. Feeling as though he may be vindicated, he took a measured step forward. Elongating what appeared to be arms, the diminutive alien individual embraced him in what he mistook for friendship. Suddenly, without warning, one of the tentacle-like arms was forced down his throat, cutting of his respiration. To his horror, he is still struggling when his abdominal cavity exploded, leaving his squirming entrails and still beating heart lying at his feet. Somehow, Carlos found the strength scream!

John, jolted out of his road weariness, spontaneously began screaming in concert, as he tried to regain control of the two ton delivery truck he had been driving for the last eight hours.

"Man! What is wrong with you? Are you trying to get us both killed?"

Slowly regaining his composure and bearings, Carlos, the older of the two so called deliverymen and the leader of the breakaway cell, sat upright and retightened his seatbelt.

"Just shut up and drive! Where are we now?"

"We are about an hour or so out!"

"Good! Very good! Let me know when we're there!"

Carlos tried to cover over the anxiety attack that he was having by acting as though nothing had happened and pretending to go back to sleep. His years of training and experience in dealing with the W.D.C., had taught him to be unflappable in every situation, but the dream had really shaken him up. That was the last thing he needed now, and that was the last thing that he would let anyone see, especially John.

"Oh, no, you don't! You can sleep and scream on your own time! Now that you're awake, I am going to stop and get some sandwiches and coffee. There won't be anything to eat in the underground, and you know the smell of the place makes me hungry."

"Really? It smells like diesel fuel and cheese!"

"Exactly!"

John pulled the truck into the next food stop he could find. A short break would do both of them some good. Both of the men had a good stretch and tried to shake off the fatigue of the hours in the cab of "the bone shaker," as they called the seemingly old and worn out cargo truck.

As the two men walked across the parking lot toward the roadside diner, the satellite phone that Carlos had been protecting with his life, began chiming quietly in his inside coat pocket, indicating an incoming encrypted text message. The exhausted Carlos retrieved it and checked the message screen making sure that no one including John could see the screen.

Arrival eminent.
Actions uncertain.
Prepare for intercept.
Good hunting.

That was exactly what Carlos and the rest of the splinter cell group were waiting for. The long months of waiting and hoping were nearing an end. Hopefully, their hard work would soon pay off.

An hour and a half later, their stomachs satisfied with super strong black coffee and greasy truck stop food and with John back at the wheel, they were nearing their destination - an underground mine and storage facility. Carved out of solid limestone by a gravel mining company over the last century, the facility covered, well actually, was covered by a thousand acres of plains land in the Northwest corner of Nebraska.

By the time the bone shaker reached its objective, there was already a line of tractor trailer rigs idling on the service road leading to the underground facilities entrance and more were sitting on the ramp that curved down and around to the opening in the ground some 80 feet below the surface. Carlos took out his cell phone and pressed the speed dial button to reach the security officer at the gate.

"Good mornin', sir. I'm a representative of Megano Data Storage with a delivery for warehouse section 32 B, room 7."

"Let me check my orders. Yes, sir, the exit ramp is clear. Just pull to the left and proceed down to the gate!"

John slowly negotiated the 30 foot long, nondescript freight hauler past the line of refrigerated transport trucks, down the ramp, carefully coming to a stop at the open guard shack window. The gate attendant spoke into the address system microphone.

"Your papers, please."

Carlos leaned out the passenger side window and handed the gate guard a manila envelope then shouted over the rumbling of diesel engines and refrigeration units.

"Here ya go, buddy! Hey! What's up with that there traffic jam?"

John almost laughed out loud.

"It's cheese day. They are all waiting to unload in cool storage. It seems like their dispatcher could space them out a little better."

John turned and looked at Carlos with a huge smile on his face.

"Cheese day! Ha! What do ya think about that, Carlos? Ha! Cheese day!"

"Just shut up and drive!"

It had been a long and difficult drive up from the secret location in Utah, but, if they got the parts there in time, they could save the world from certain Alien domination. It had been a little over 36 hours since the word came down that They were coming.

The team had been working toward and planning for this "Event" for several years but hoped that there was time to get it all together. With the parts that they had on the truck, their "Mega Weapon" would be complete. The next few hours were to be critical to the whole operation. If the information they received was correct, their only window for success would be opening sometime in the next day or so.

"Hey, Carlos, do you remember how this place looked the last time we were here?"

"Yes, John! You talk about it all the time!"

"I know, but it is so cool! It looks like a dragon's mouth."

During the winter months when the ambient temperature is cold enough, the mouth of the man-made cavern is nearly obscured by an eerie fog, caused by the warmth and humidity of the mine colliding with the cold dry air of the atmosphere above. On really cold days, the fog extended for several yards inside the facility, making the already close quarters of the underground corridors all the more treacherous.

A modern engineering marvel, the mining operation was gigantic by anyone's standards. The solid limestone ceiling was some 40 feet above the floor and supported by huge 30 foot diameter pillars strategically left when the mine had been expanded over the years. Illuminated by flood lights hanging from the ceiling placed a hundred feet apart, the man-made cavern had a feeling of security and secrecy. The space between the support pillars was enough for two full-sized diesel rigs to easily pass one another with plenty of room to spare.

On either side of the corridors were rooms, each with its own office front and hanger-type doors. The rooms varied from several hundred square feet of floor space to an acre or two, depending on the renters' needs. Some of the office fronts were decorated with the company's logo but most were not. Identified only by a very large number painted on the façade of the room and on the floor in the corresponding loading zone, there was no telling what was being stored behind those doors.

The only security stipulations were that each load coming in and out had to be signed for by the proper agent proving that it belonged to the correct company. No loads were checked for content, and that was a perfect situation for doing covert work. The storage facility managers didn't care what was being stored in the rooms, as long as they got paid.

The bone shaker's exhaust echoed off the limestone walls as Carlos and John slowly descended the ramp to the bottom of the mine. After making another two turns, 10 minutes later they had covered the 200 yards to where a big white number 7 was painted on the door and the floor beneath it.

"Home sweet home! Can you just smell that cheese?"

***

Behind Jupiter

Roy boarded his saucer shaped shuttle and slipped into the jelly-like liner of his flight pod. Before lifting off, he prepared himself mentally and emotionally for the challenges set before him. Each of the ships had at its core of operation any number of flight pods, depending on the size and purpose of the spacecraft. The pods themselves looked similar to a bathtub, oval in shape and crystal clear. Inside the pod was the "Jell," a genetically engineered living organism. The Jell was in this case pale blue but could be changed to any color imaginable. Pale blue was just Roy's personal preference. The flight pod's Jell was a direct interface with the occupants mind and body. From inside the protection of the pod, the body functions were minimized bringing them to unperceivable levels and thereby allowing the cognitive abilities of the brain to be maximized. This gave one the ability to think hundreds of thousands of times faster than normal. Interfaced with the brain of the ship through the Jell, the Primary or Pilot had total control of the ship's flight path, speed, illumination, and communications. The brain of the ship was more organic than the Jell and was in actuality a brain grown for this specific purpose. The brain had no independent thought of its own, only serving as an amplifier for the thoughts and actions of the Primary.

Roy loved to fly these machines because all he had to do was think and the ship instantaneously responded. His awareness was so enhanced that at thousands of miles per hour his mind kept up as though the ship was flying in slow motion. In the event of a miscalculation by the Pilot, a collision with an object of any kind would be nearly impossible due to the force of the Bymagnetis Stabilizer. Although such an encounter was highly unlikely, Roy or one of the other humans would most likely be involved. The reason being was that the brain of the ship was a perfect match to the nonhuman physiology, but the human mind and body were patched into the system for convenience sake. The truth was that the Friends did it all for Roy.

After a couple of loops inside the great ship, the shuttle made its way out through a portal and headed for Earth. One other small craft soon followed. As per Earth's government's request, they would have to be careful that no one on the planet could catch a glimpse of them. It was the only way to maintain what the military called "plausible deniability."

In the 30 years since the First Visitation, improved mechanical tracking actuators and mainframe computer drives on Earth's telescopes made it possible to precisely track and photograph any unusual object in the Solar system, not to mention satellite reconnaissance. The three shuttles swiftly made their approach to Earth, cautiously keeping the planets and, finally, Earth's moon between them and direct line of sight. The ships were playing an interstellar game of hide and seek.

It would take only six hours to traverse the 390,500,000 miles between Jupiter and Earth's moon. To Roy, it seemed like an eternity, even though the shuttles were traveling at nearly six times the speed of light. The little ships were rather slow compared to the gigantic mega cruiser that could travel at thousands of times their rate.

Upon entering a planet's atmosphere, the shuttles could not be detected by any electronic detection devices including Earth's radar, but they could still be spotted with the naked eye, telescope, or video surveillance (that is if the Primary didn't jam the video signal). The small ships were also equipped with a camouflage of sorts. The light from above would be transferred to the bottom of the ship and vice versa from bottom to top, making the ship virtually invisible from above or below. All that could be detected while in stealth mode was a slight distortion around the peripheries of the flight bubble. The ships wouldn't even leave a shadow in full sunlight unless they wanted to be detected, as in the first Visitation. This time, they would fly at night and without lights to avoid raising any suspicion. The truth of the matter was, when it came to unidentified flying objects, if people on the ground ever saw anything, it was of Earthly origin. The shuttle ship silently dropped out of the night sky, quickly deposited Roy and a survival module onto the hospital roof, and then retreated to the dark side of the moon, rejoining the other two waiting shuttles.

The survival module was designed to conceal and protect its occupant for several hundred years, if need be, by slowing the occupant's life functions to almost zero and by being completely undetectable by any means except touch (the avoidance technology took care of any possibility of physical detection by simply moving out of harm's way).

The use of the module would give Roy all the time he needed. His clandestine plan was to stay concealed during the day and visit with Ronnie at night when he would be less apt to run into any problems. Roy may have had all the time in the world, but Ronnie's condition made it imperative that he convince her of his intensions sooner than later. Time was running out for her.

Roy touched a sensor on the outside of the module and instantly his one piece silver metallic flight suit was transformed into Earth time appropriate street wear comprised of a pair of running shoes, blue jeans, and a red pullover. He took a second to check his hair and facial appearance. To his delight, Roy now appeared to be the same age as his eldest son Brad, not a dead ringer, but close enough to fool the nursing staff. Brad, at that time, was a little older than Roy was when he went missing.

He touched another sensor and the module went into cloak mode, making it completely invisible to the naked eye. Roy knew that, in case of an emergency, he could access the survival module minutes sooner than his awaiting shuttle could reach his location. In a disaster, even seconds could mean the difference between life and death.

Roy was drawn to the edge of the hospital's roof by the sounds of traffic and the glow of the city lights ten stories below. Across the street lay an air base with military aircraft coming and going all night and day. Roy's shoes crunched on the gravel of the roof, a sound he hadn't heard in a long, long time. Roy took a deep breath and coughed. He had been breathing filtered air while he was away and hadn't re-acclimated to Earth air yet. The odor of the city was so thick that he could taste it. *Roy was home*!

***

Otis

Otis, a 70 year old retired aeronautics engineer, just sat there bolt upright in his easy chair. He was living a very comfortable retirement. His many years of saving and investing wisely had paid off well. Otis was able to afford a very nice beach-front home with all the amenities, including a house keeper and private duty nurse. His life was a model of peace and safety. Although safe from the turmoil and dangers of the outside world, Otis was not isolated from the ravages of the ageing mind. Some days were better than others, but, on the worst of them, reality got a little skewed. He was shocked and mesmerized at what was transpiring on the screen of his fifty-one inch plasma television. For most of his life, he had been aware that there was a possibility that extraterrestrial Visitation could be more than science fiction. During his long career, Otis had heard a myriad of harrowing accounts from military and commercial pilots alike. Now, it was apparent to him that it was more than a possibility. Chills ran up and down his back as he watched one after another interstellar craft breach the atmosphere and disperse around the globe.

***

Aleutian Islands, Alaska

The sky was clear and the weather balmy as Sylvia and her companions hiked along a winding mountain road somewhere in the deep forests of Colorado. The air was so fresh and crisp that she could almost taste it. Sylvia couldn't remember ever being there before, but it felt like home to her. The deep feeling of contentment was almost as thick as the scent of the pines wafting through the ancient forest that stretched for hundreds of miles on either side of the road.

It was beginning to get dark, and the trio had a long way to go before they would be safe. Now, for some unknown reason, the small group of travelers was hiking across one of the largest cities in the world. No one spoke as they made their way through darkened alleyways and across dimly lit thoroughfares, cautiously trudging their way to who knows where. The other two figures accompanying Sylvia were very familiar, even though she couldn't quite make out their faces. Once again, there was a deep feeling of contentment, an ease, a joy in being on this trip with these loved ones.

Eventually, Sylvia began to get the strong feeling that her traveling companions were her parents, even though her mother was hundreds of miles away in the hospital with heart failure, and her father hadn't been in her life since she was a little girl. Maybe this was a repressed memory or a manifestation of a bruised psyche, but she didn't really care. This was the best feeling that she had had in years.

Sylvia held tight to the other's hands as they strolled their way down the sidewalk that ran alongside the main avenue leading to the city's center. From Sylvia's vantage point, she could see the lights of the city twinkling through the smog that hung like low clouds, obscuring the biggest part of the sprawling metropolis. The traffic in the city was horrendous, and Sylvia was glad to be walking with them instead of driving.

As the little family trudged down the street toward their unknown destination, Sylvia stopped momentarily to pick a beautiful orange and black Tiger Lilly from a flower bed haphazardly growing unattended between the side walk and a parking lot, carelessly letting go of her traveling partners' hands. As she looked up, she suddenly realized that she was alone. Fear instantly swept over her. Contentment was replaced with terror, joy with sadness. Sylvia ran from person to person along the street asking everyone she met if they had seen them, franticly screaming out their names.

Sylvia awoke with a start. A wave of pure sorrow washing over her; she lay there crying for the better part of an hour. That is why she tried to sleep as little as possible, but, to her regret, pure exhaustion had finally overcome her. Wiping the tears from her face, Sylvia turned on some music and tried to shake off the anxiety. She was once again safe in her steel reinforced fortress hidey hole at the top of the world.

Chapter 2
Abandonment

Back at the hospital in southern California, Brad's mother was calm again for now. As soon as he was sure that his mother was fast asleep again, he slumped into the overstuffed easy chair that often had been utilized as a sleeper. Brad was exhausted from the experience. The incident had left him with many questions and concerns, but underneath it all was an abiding anger focused on the man that should have been there by his mother's side. Brad slid his smart phone out of his uniform jacket pocket, and touched the icon labeled "Selmail".

selsmith@skywatch.gov:
Sylvia, mom had a rough morning and had to be sedated. She was confused and delusional. The doctors say that she is stable, but I feel that she is slipping away. Come as soon as you can. Brad
P.S. Pass this along to Toby.

colbradfordsmith@flyfast.gov:
Good to hear from you, brother. I am trying to make arrangements to get off this rock as soon as the weather breaks. Tell Mama that I love her and will be there soon. Also, tell her that I am planning to move home to be with her. I will call Toby and pass on the message. I will twist his arm and get him home too! Love you, Sylvia

Brad stayed at his mother's bedside for another two hours, until it was about time to return to base. After a short conference with the attending doctor and the floor nurses, he decided to catch a quick snack at the diner across the street before returning to base. Crossing the street in front of the hospital was always a tricky situation, but Brad knew that he had to be extra careful when crossing during rush hour. Some impatient people just wanting to get home often took dangerous chances to save a few minutes sitting at a red light. Over the years, several pedestrians had been badly injured and at least one killed by motorists running the stop light. It wouldn't have been a problem at all, except that the hospital parking lot closest to the cardiac wing was full as usual so he had to park in the diner's side lot under a tree.

Brad was still breathing heavily from the sprint across the crosswalk as he slid into his favorite seat, but, due to the Air Force physical training regimen, he recovered quickly. Brad was so preoccupied that he barely noticed the beautiful, young, cleanly dressed waitress as he ordered his usual - a burger with everything on it, onion rings, and strawberry malt. While waiting for his order, Brad thought about his mother's hopeless condition and the inevitable emptiness that her death would bring. He closed his eyes to rest them after the long day at his dying mother's side. Brad didn't realize that he had dozed off until a tinkling sound aroused him. When the cheery waitress arrived at the table with his food, she had tapped the side of his malt glass with a spoon.

"Are you okay, honey pie?"

"Yes, Ma'am. Just a little bit tired, I guess."

"Well, just relax and enjoy your meal! If you need anything else, just give a whistle, sweetie!"

The young woman winked at him before walking away. Brad knew that her friendliness was most likely due to the fifties motif of the diner. The popular thought that neighborhood diners during the 1950s were all populated with gorgeous young waitresses wearing tight fitting white uniforms accentuated with big red bows in their hair and nylon hose with a perfectly strait seam running down the back of the legs was for the most part untrue, but he liked it very much anyway. He later responded by leaving her a generous tip, which was the point of her performance, although her kindness and willingness to serve was nonetheless very sincere.

Brad wasn't very hungry, but he finished his food and malt anyway knowing that it probably would be several hours before he had an opportunity to eat again. He sat there thinking to himself how it sure would be nice to have Toby and Sylvia home, not just to give him a break, and man did he need a break, but he really did miss them. Brad leaned back into the overstuffed booth bench seat and stared up at "Her" picture on the wall across from his table.

"At least, I've always got you! Don't I, old girl?"

Thinking about Mary always lifted his spirits, and seeing her smiling face in the photo hanging on the wall of the diner always made his day. At least she wouldn't abandon him! He brushed away the feelings of melancholy; after all, his brother and sister had their own lives to live.

***

Toby

Twelve hundred nautical miles southeast of Madagascar in the southern Indian Ocean, twenty eight degrees south of the equator on an unnamed volcanic island, the ground beneath the remote encampment began to shudder only so slightly. The instruments had been recording tremors two to three miles deep on and off for months, but now the tremors were beginning to register on the surface. The carbon dioxide levels had been steadily rising over the last two days, and that was never a good sign unless you actually wanted to witness up close one of nature's most wonderfully violent cataclysms.

The ancient extinct volcano was slowly waking from a thousand year sleep. The island itself was relatively young, being formed only about three or four thousand years ago. The volcanic island had cooled and went dormant after a thousand years of sporadic diminishing eruptions. Now the island was beautifully covered in lush vegetation and home to many species of birds, lizards, snakes, and other creatures that had been blown there from distant islands or hitchhiked a ride on visiting boats and ships that had frequented the, now evacuated, picturesque fishing village located in the islands only cove. It was a true tropical paradise, but that was about to change.

This was what Dr. Tobias Smith (Roy and Ronnie's middle child) had waited and worked for most of his life. At a young age, he had become incredibly interested in volcanoes. Toby knew full well that his near obsession had been sparked by the loss of his father. Where had he gone? Why did he leave? Was he still alive? What did that huge pile of dirt in the living room mean? Was it a sculpture of a volcano or just the result of a complete mental breakdown? There had been a slip of the tongue by his mother once, something about Devil's Tower, but he could never get her to discuss it. One summer, unbeknownst to his mother, Toby and a group of college friends took a road trip to the monument, but the experience only increased his curiosity. If his father's departure had not been the result of a psychotic break, then it had to be important.

Toby had been searching for something all of his life. There was no mountain too high or cave to deep for him to search. His chosen profession had taken him all around the globe, but he knew deep down that he was actually searching for his father. Toby had never given up hope that someday he would find him and make him explain where he had been or, at the very least, discover the circumstances of his demise.

After the move to California, Toby had gotten deeply involved in a new organization called "World Explorers." World Explorers.org was created for boys aged eight to adulthood through a grant from an anonymous donor. The "X boys," as they came to be known, were not only trained in wilderness survival and extreme exploration techniques but were each expected to achieve and maintain a 3.5 G.P.A. or better. The X boys were each to be paired with a mentor whose expertise was in the area closest matching that boy's aptitude and interest. Because of his near obsession with volcanoes, Toby was paired with a retired professor of geology, who in his younger days had worked for the world geological survey specializing in volcanology.

Throughout the years, there had been many teachers and mentors, all guiding him along the way. Toby knew in his heart that he was one of the luckiest men in the world. He had done the work and put in the time to earn the degrees, nothing had been given to him except the opportunity. All he had to do was to reach out and take it!

***

Barry
Northeastern Wyoming

The stars were twinkling brilliantly against the blackness of the summer night sky. A sweet aroma of honeysuckle blossoms delicately combining with the perfume of a myriad of other wild flowers was so thick that Barry could almost taste it. The moon was bright and full, hanging in space like a gigantic pearl, illuminating the countryside with a surreal aura. Within the one hundred and forty acre woodlot adjoining the back of the only home that young Barry had ever known, the night had come alive with the chirping of crickets, the croaking of tree frogs, and the songs of night birds. A gentle breeze was whispering through the trees causing them to wave slightly back and forth in a delicate ballet. The sun-dried cornstalks in the adjacent farm field fluttered in the gentle wind, sounding like so many millions of migrating butterflies beating their wings in chorus as they made their way franticly to their mating grounds. It was one of those nights that would bring a feeling of pure peace and contentment to the soul of any country boy's heart.

Barry was running joyously and with total abandonment in the moon glow between the shadows of the trees, chasing after his new found Friends. He didn't know who they were or, for that matter, what they were, but they were the most interesting things he had ever seen. Barry's new found Friends were a little taller than his five year old frame, whitish grey in the moon light, with large dark eyes that seemed to look into his soul. The fact that they could stretch their little bodies at will like silly putty made them irresistible to Barry.

As the chase progressed, he could hear his mother, Jillian, crying out his name.

"Barry! Hare-reee!!! Where are you Barry?"

Breaking into a clearing, Barry could see his little Friends waiting for him. Several of the diminutive creatures were standing in front of the most beautiful object he had ever seen. Brightly lit and pulsating with a rainbow of vivid colors, the cone shaped ship hovered silently, drawing Barry to it like a moth to a flame.

Soon after, he discovered that he was flying. Barry could inexplicably see in all directions at one time as though he had a thousand eyes. He felt as though he was somehow floating on the breeze, like a helium filled balloon accidently set free by a careless child. Barry could see the stars, the moon, the fields, his house, and his mother standing there with that horrible look on her face. She was still screaming out his name as Barry and his Friends shot spaceward, accompanied by several other brightly lit, oddly shaped objects.

Barry, even though he was a small child, was feeling totally at ease in his new surroundings as the oddly shaped craft shot skyward. The ship immediately gained altitude, leaving Earth's atmosphere as the screams of his mother quickly faded. As time went on, darkness began to close in and anxiety began to well up in Barry's mind. His pulse began to quicken and breathing became difficult. For some inexplicable reason, he soon found himself slowly drifting into darkness, falling down, down, down, faster, and faster into an abyss that had instantaneously opened before him. Barry began frantically grasping in the blackness for anything to slow his decent but he was unable to find anything substantial to grab on to. In desperation, he screamed for help. His cry was in vain, no one could hear him.

***

Toby was standing on the summit of the tallest mountain in the range, trying to focus his telescope on the figure of a man that was slowly walking across a meadow more than five miles away. The more he focused his eyes on the illusive silhouette, the more the image blurred. Toby leaned away from the instrument and listened to a distant voice emanating from the valley below. He once again peered through the eye piece hoping to recognize the strangely familiar person that was now waving his arms in a friendly manner. As he looked and listened intently, the faint voice began to become clear. Straining with all that he had within him, he was finally able to make out what the apparition was trying to say.

"I'm coming, Toby. I'll be there soon. I love you son, don't give up."

A huge dragon fly landed on Toby's nose, very rudely disturbing his sleep. He swatted the insect away, nearly falling out of his cot. Even though Toby was a man's man, the dream had touched him deeply, and he was overcome with emotion. He lay back in his bed and wept.

***

Las Vegas, Nevada

The landing gear clunked into place as the airliner made its final approach. Sam Drocer woke with a start; he couldn't believe that he had been asleep for most of the flight from

Marfa. Rubbing the sleep from his bloodshot brown eyes, he yawned and stretched in his economy class seat. Sam was glad to be getting home. It had been a hard two weeks of taking statements and sky watching. He had been in Texas investigating another supposed U.F.O. outbreak. There had been plenty of blurry photos and jiggly video to watch, but, once again, it appeared that he was too late for the live event.

Why was he still doing this? To be honest with himself, he wasn't quite sure. Other than an encounter that he had as a child, he hadn't been able to actually document a sighting himself. It seemed that he was always a day late and a dollar short.

As a child, his family had moved around a lot. The story as it was gathered by Sam (he was only one year old when the move was made) was that his father was moving their family from Missouri to California in search of a better life, when their "old clunker" broke down in Colorado. In actuality, Sam found out 30 years later that the family car wasn't an old clunker after all; it had been a brand new Ford sedan. The problem had been that his father was trying to pull a 36 foot long mobile home with it when the overtaxed engine blew up somewhere around Denver. Having no job, little money, and no way to replace the engine, they were stuck. Luckily, Sam had relatives living in the area, which wasn't that odd. He had relatives just about everywhere. The Drocer family history went way back, including one that had fought in the War of Independence.

Sam was very young at the time, but he remembered those days with great fondness. Mr. Drocer eventually found work with a highway construction crew, but that would mean that the family would have to follow the highway as it progressed across the mountains. Finding work was difficult to do back then, and the family had to go where ever the work was, that is, if they wanted to stay together.

It was one big adventure to a little boy with a big imagination. Eventually, the mobile homes got bigger, and the family truck had to get more powerful to pull them around and over the Rocky Mountains. During those years as trailer gypsies, the young family found themselves wandering from one town to the next. Mister Drocer and Sam's older brother Bruce were so accomplished at moving the family castle that they could have it unplugged, disconnected, unblocked, and ready to move in less than two hours. There had been other cars and trucks to pull their home around the state, but the one that Sam remembered the most was Big Red, a 1958, three quarter ton, dually, Chevy truck with a homemade steel flat bed that his father built. To this day, the spectacular cackling of the truck's homemade mufflers as they pulled their fifty foot long, ten foot wide mobile home up and down the mountain passes was one of the many childhood memories that Sam cherished.

In one small town on the high mountain plains of Colorado, one of many that the young family found themselves temporarily sojourning in, Sam had an encounter that relentlessly haunted him, even in adulthood. At age five, he was playing by himself in front of their family's mobile home when an object appeared in the sky. Even though Sam was at such an innocent age, he remembered very distinctly what he saw. The object seared in his memory was round like the moon but had a ring around it similar to Saturn. The object appeared to be much larger than the moon would be in comparison and seemed to be in the neighborhood, so to speak. There was no gap between the ring and the globe-shaped portion of the object, and the ring was tilted, so that the whole surface could be seen. He remembered standing there, staring, and suddenly it was gone! The encounter was something he would never forget. Fifty some odd years later, it was as sharp in his memory as if it had happened yesterday.

In his never-ending quest for the truth, Sam had become an accomplished wild life and landscape photographer. The opportunities afforded him by the sale of his photographs made it possible to pursue his real passion, UFOlogy. If only he could get one definitive photograph, he could die happy.

Sam knew far too well that if he was going to get conclusive evidence of alien visitation, he would have to do it soon, while he still could. Although he still felt relatively good, the inoperable cancer growing in his brain was not going to wait much longer before the chemotherapy, set to start soon, would tear his life apart. All he needed was to catch a break, to be in the right place at the right time.

The airliner's tires barked as it touched down at the Las Vegas airport. Sam looked out the small window beside his seat catching a glimpse of his reflection. "I really have to get some rest," he thought to himself. Sam ran his fingers through his wavy copper-hued hair, massaged the back of his neck, and yawned again. He could see the distant mountains shimmering through the heat waves emanating off of the desert floor. He wasn't looking forward to getting out into the heat but, all in all, it was good to be back. Sam was feeling his age as he walked down the tunnel ramp to the entry gate. It had been a long bumpy flight, and he was ready for a rest. His steps gained energy as he covered the last few yards to the egress into the terminal. He always looked forward to coming home. Las Vegas was several miles from his home on the Extraterrestrial Highway, and sometimes Sam thought about moving into town. With his illness, it was sometimes pure drudgery to make the drive. Then there was the Susann situation. Sam was between a rock and a hard place with her.

He wasn't yet sure if he was falling in love with her, but he did know that he admired her very much. The problem was their age difference and his medical condition. Until he knew how the chemotherapy was going to turn out, it didn't matter about their age difference anyway.

The airliner bumped to a stop next to Terminal Gate 7 and Sam breathed a sigh of relief. After getting the "okay" from the flight attendants, Sam and the rest of the passengers gathered their belongings and slowly trudged down the aisle to the jet-way mobile bridge. The heat in the tunnel felt like it had to be over a hundred degrees, not bad for Las Vegas. The automatic double doors at the opening of the egress portico slowly swung open, and there she stood! Sam's heart skipped a beat as he resisted the urge to take her in his arms and kiss her.

"Welcome home, Sam! Have a good trip?"

"Just another wild goose chase I'm afraid, Susann!"

"You will find what you are looking for soon, Sam. I have faith in you!"

"I appreciate your optimism, Susann."

"We can talk about it later if you want. I am getting off soon!"

"I'm sorry, Susann, I appreciate the offer, but this trip was a disaster and I'm bone tired. I will be coming back into town in a couple of days. If you want, we can get together then."

Sam knew that he was being less than honest with Susann, but he didn't know what else to do.

***

Jim and Connie
On the island

For Jim and Connie Friend, this trip was a dream come true, an adventure of a lifetime. Jim, a thin, average height, sixty year old man sporting a farmer's tan and month old vacation beard, had retired two years earlier from a long successful career as a residential home designer. He and Connie had been somewhat at loose ends, so, when the opportunity came up to spend several months chaperoning a group of college interns on an research project in the Indian Ocean, it was a no brainer. Even though Jim was a white collar professional, he was a real outdoorsman at heart and tried to go exploring in the national forest near his home in Middle America whenever possible. He loved the smell of the trees, the rumble of his four wheel drive A.T.V. as he scrambled up and down the mountain trails, and the pure sense of freedom that it gave him. Being able to take a trip to the other side of the globe with the love of his life, his wife of over 40 years, was wonderful beyond words, but finding out that there would be A.T.V.s, well, that was the cherry on top!

If there was a perfect woman for Jim, it was Connie. A little bit taller than Jim (he would never admit to it), she had beautiful silver-blond hair that was never out of place. A medium build, self-assured, self-effacing, stylish woman on the surface, but a real tom boy underneath, she was the real asset on this trip. Although she was in her late fifties (she wouldn't admit to be older than 39 and always said "a woman that would tell her age would tell anything"), she was still young at heart and quite active for her age. Connie could host a formal dinner affair one weekend and then go deer hunting the next. Between the two of them, they were up to any challenge. There were three female and three male interns on this trip, and, although they were all intelligent dedicated scholars, they were still young people, and there would be no running amok on Connie's watch. To pursue anything other than volcanic research could call down "the wrath of Conn," as Jim called it. She could be tough when she needed to be, but the kids, as she called them, all called her Mom.

The diverse group of female interns on the research expedition was of all shapes and descriptions. Feonia, an average height, well proportioned brunette, considered to be the prettiest of the group of women on the island, was an exchange student from Brigadoon, Scotland, a small village in the Scottish Highlands.

Then there was Dolly, a petite, redhead with an adventuresome spirit and fiery temper, if pushed too hard. She came from the Ozark hill country, growing up in an impoverished back woods community with two brothers and six sisters. Connie knew that in a pinch, cute little Dolly could handle herself. Early on in their adventure, one of the sailors onboard the supply ship tried to steal a kiss and, in response to the intrusion, she knocked him out cold.

Last, but not least, Angel, a blond haired beauty, was the real scholar on the crew, but to most people's surprise, her real passion was in working on all types and descriptions of internal combustion engines. Angel was the one to locate the plugged fuel filter on the supply ship when it unexpectedly shut down in the middle of the Indian Ocean.

Of the three male interns, Junior (as the others called him but nobody knew why) was the strongest of all the men on the island. Blond hair, 6 feet tall, he was just one of those guys that had a natural strength to him physically and mentally. Connie knew that Junior was an honorable man; it was the girls that she was keeping an eye on.

Chase, the most outgoing of the "boys," as Connie called them, was 5' 6" with curly auburn hair. He was highly intelligent, analytical, and precise. He was a gentle soul but seemed to always have something to prove.

A fourth degree black belt by the time he was sixteen, Sito was a true enigma, the medium height blonde looked nothing like the other members of his family. Adopted as a newborn into a traditional Japanese family, he was named after the family's patriarch, a very honorable rice farmer. Sito believed deeply in his name sake's motto, "The weapon that is hidden strikes with devastation," a rather odd saying for a simple rice farmer. No one had a clue to his abilities.

"Come on, Connie, everybody is waiting! The boat will think we aren't coming."

"Alright! Alright! I'm coming! They won't leave without unloading."

After another half hour, the convoy of A.T.V.s finally got started down the treacherous, winding trail leading down to the coastline. Jim was the real explorer of the group, but he always let someone else lead the way. Connie thought that it was a method of instilling confidence in the kids, but, truth be known, it was all about spider webs.

After an hour of hard riding, slowly making their way through the most beautiful tropical vistas imaginable, the convoy popped out of the jungle onto the pristine black sand beach fronting the half moon cove. The ocean was calm and the waves were gently lapping against the rocky shoreline encompassing nearly the entire island, other than the cove, accessible only to birds and lizards. It was another phenomenal day in the Indian Ocean. The sun was shining brightly through a cloudless sky, bringing the temperature to almost 90 degrees, but there was a cool ocean breeze gently blowing making the weather nearly perfect. Jim, Connie, and the rest of the research group knew far too well to enjoy the good weather while they could. The weather, like many other things on the island, was subject to change at a moment's notice.

"Where's the boat? It's supposed to be here!"

"Don't worry, Connie. It will be here soon."

"Oh! There it is on the horizon. At this rate, we'll have to spend the night here."

"That's okay, I like sleeping on the beach."

"You can sleep with the crabs if you want to Mr. Jim Friend, but, as for me, there's a hammock in the grass shack for me."

"Where's your sense of adventure, Connie?"

"Look around, Jim, we are standing on one of the most obscure islands in the Indian Ocean, created by a volcano, hundreds of miles from anything, depending for our lives on a boat captained by someone that probably doesn't even own a watch or, for that matter, a calendar, and you're getting bored! Did I mention that this is a volcano that might erupt at any time?"

"Point taken! Tomorrow the guys and I are going on a hog hunt!"

"The last time you guys went, you hunted for two days for a hog, and all you got was a cut on your head and a sprained ankle. I don't think hogs even exist on this rock."

"I am pretty sure that I heard hogs in the jungle."

"Well, I'm pretty sure that you imagined them, so there! It's like they say, 'When pigs fly.'"

"You'll be sorry when we are all eating imaginary barbecue pork sandwiches. As a matter of fact, I saw a couple of them fly over early this morning. So there! Ha!"

"Ha, yourself, Jungle Jim!"

Jim and Connie had a funny way of arguing over little things, but, when it came to larger issues, they stuck together like glue.

The supply boat anchored about a hundred yards from the beach, where the cove was deep enough to keep from running aground. It was an old rusty tub called Neptune's Girlfriend. Actually, it could be classified as a small ship. At ninety feet long, it was large enough to comfortably cross the nearly 1,200 mile expanse of open-ocean between the island and the nearest supply port. In order to get the supplies that the team needed to do their work and make their lives easier, they would have to hand transfer them from the ship to a twenty foot long motor launch and then carry them down a rickety old dock to the supply hut and waiting A.T.V.s. Connie was right, by the time that the research team got the supplies off of the ship and onto the A.T.V.s, it would be too late to start back to the highland observation base on the other side of the island.

After a good supper of canned meat sautéed in coconut milk, something that passed for potatoes baked on the grill covering a small fire on the beach, and some kind of noodles that looked like worms, the team started wandering off to bed. It had been a long, hard day, and that hammock was sounding better all the time.

Jim lay in his hammock thinking about what Connie had said. Of course, she was right! She was always right! He came to the realization that it is up to each person to keep their mind busy, in paradise or behind a desk. As Jim slowly swung in his hammock bed, looking at the moon reflecting off of the crystal clear waters of the cove, he still wished for something exciting to happen, maybe the volcano would erupt! He drifted off to sleep thinking, "maybe tomorrow."

***

Las Vegas, Nevada

Susann Roberts was a petit, auburn haired, blue eyed, pretty young woman of 23 years. Standing there in her airline receptionist uniform, she looked like a movie star to Sam. There was something special about her, the way she smiled and touched his hand when she was talking to him. The way she always seemed to be excited to see him. The way she really seemed to care about the ridiculous lifestyle that he was living. Was there something there or was he just imagining things?

Sam was desperately lonely, all of his immediate family had passed, the last one a few years back. He wanted to spend time with Susann, but he knew that just being lonely wasn't enough to base a relationship on. Although he cared for her very much, the worsening of his cancer made it a path that he felt he shouldn't go down.

"This is crazy!" He told himself. There is no way that a beautiful woman like Susann could be interested in him. Sure, they had a few common interests, the love of photography and of the outdoors but would that be enough to build a life on? Build a life on, that was exactly the problem! How much life did he have left? At 48, Sam was already more than twice her age of 23, and there was the cancer to consider. He couldn't put her through that, no matter how he felt about her. Sam couldn't bear to think of it any longer so he gave Susann a warm but detached good bye, again resisting the urge to give her a kiss.

As Sam slowly walked away, Susann could see that he was very tired, more tired than she had ever seen him before.

"That guy has it bad for you, Susann!"

"I don't know about that, Annie, but I sure wish it was true! Every time I feel like we are connecting, he pulls away. There seems to be something that causes him to put on the brakes"

"Maybe it's his age; he is old enough to be your father."

"That doesn't matter to me. The reason that I don't date men my age is that they are too unpredictable, you know that! Remember Brad, and Joe, and Fred, and well, the list goes on. A man like Sam is more settled. He knows what he wants and where he is going. All I need is the opportunity to explain it to him. I know that he has a house somewhere out on the ET highway, but I can't seem to muster the courage to ask him exactly where he lives. We have even gone out to eat a couple of times, and for some odd reason it just never came up."

"Maybe you could just take a little drive and "bump" into him somewhere between Los Vegas and the mountains, you know! It could happen."

"You read too many romance novels, Annie! What am I supposed to do, chase him down like some love struck teenager? What I am going to do tomorrow is wander out into the foot hills and take some wildlife photos for the Nevada wildlife photography show next month."

"Oh! So you're hunting the desert Jackalope again! Or, let me guess, Bigfoot. Or... Maybe you have bigger game in mind?"

"Oh, you're rotten! No, you goof! Peace and quiet is what I will be mostly hunting. There is nothing like the peace and solitude that you can find in the desert. Besides, I think he lives somewhere out in the desert off the extraterrestrial highway. The odds of just bumping into him out there are a billion to one. You should come with me some time. You would love it."

"No way, Jungle Jane. I get all the solitude I need on the strip. Besides, three's a crowd if you find Bigfoot, that is!"

"Okay, okay, all I know is that, when I'm alone in the wilderness, I am not searching faces on the street trying to find Sam!"

***

In the Underground
Carlos slowly crawled down out of the truck cab and meticulously typed in the security code for the door opener. The door creaked and groaned as it rose to its full open position. John pulled the truck into the opening two full truck

lengths and then stopped just short of a painted screen that blocked the entire passageway, looking very convincingly from the corridor outside like the room beyond was empty. It was very low tech but also very effective. As soon as the big steel door closed behind the truck, Carlos tapped in a code on his smart phone, and the screen slid to one side revealing, among other things, two men sitting at a small table playing cards. The bigger of the two turned around in his chair and shouted.

"Well, if it isn't Danger Man and his sidekick, Rambo!"

"Yeah, like your code name is any better- Popeye! Why don't you, John, and Nikola just get to work offloading the bone shaker?"

The entire cell team had chosen code names for themselves, some after people or characters that they admired or, in Carlos's case, one that was so outrageously opposite that he believed that no one would ever discover his true identity. Choosing the screen name of a failed political candidate was undoubtedly the funniest thing that the other team members had ever known their consistently austere and demanding leader to do. The oldest of the cell and the group leader, code name Carlos Danger, was a tall thin man in his late fifties with narrow set green eyes and nearly white hair, although he had recently dyed it dark brown and wore glaucoma style sunglasses as part of his disguise. Carlos also had a habit of trying to talk like a southern country boy as part of his disguise but was clueless that he just sounded stupid.

The youngest member of the group, code name John Rambo, took his moniker from a moving picture character that had extraordinary strength and fighting abilities, none of which he himself possessed. John was a fairly short, red haired, doe bellied, loudmouth who liked to joke around and antagonize anyone within a 30 foot circle. At the time, he had a black eye from pushing Popeye a little too hard. He was on the team for his loyalty and medical expertise, not his fighting ability or personality. The four men generally got along well, but, in joking around, sometimes he went too far. At least after the incident, John knew his limits with Popeye, who had responded with a sincere "sorry dude" and a man hug.

John had dropped out of medical school in his fourth year to assist in what he considered to be a higher calling. He believed deeply in Carlo's cause to save mankind. After all, if there weren't any humans left on the planet, there would be no need for doctors.

Popeye on the other hand, even at age 40, was a force to be reckoned with, a real warrior. His six foot tall frame was sculpted, bronzed, and scarred from years of Navy Seal training and active combat. Growing his coal black hair into a Mohawk was something that he had decided to do for shock effect. Combine all that with his piercing bluish-grey eyes that gave him the look of a predator, and, at a glance, you could tell that he was no one to be trifled with. Although he had the look of a killer, the real man was patriotic, loyal, and compassionate.

Like most Navy Seals, Popeye had tattoos. On his upper right chest, he wore the typical badge of the naval warrior class, portraying an eagle with wings spread, roosting on an anchor with a flint lock pistol in one talon and a trident in the other. Portrayed on his massive right bicep was the cartoon character Olive Oyl, and on his left was a portrait of Swee'Pea from the 1930s cartoon series, Popeye. John and Tesla thought that he had the tattoos of Olive and Swee'Pea because he chose the code name Popeye, but, in actuality, he chose it because of the tattoos. During one of his tours of duty he became highly decorated for his action in a war zone. He went in under fire and rescued a woman and a child from certain death, acquiring several wounds himself and barely escaping with his life. He had them inked on his arms level with his heart and, unbeknownst to any of his friends, he still kept in contact, giving them financial and emotional support from afar. There was a lot more to Popeye than anyone knew.

Last, but not least, was code named Tesla after the genius inventor and electrical engineer, Nicola Tesla. 6 feet tall, very thin, and 38 years old, Tesla looked very similar to the 6' 2", 140 pound, historical character except for his pale green eyes (Nicola had light blue eyes) and his dark brown hair and mustache (Nicola's was jet black). Tesla, the cell member, had an extraordinary intellect, especially when it came to the field of electronics and computer programming, making him extremely valuable in the effort to save the world. The fact was that, without him, there was no effort. Although he was very intelligent, Tesla himself had to admit that he couldn't hold a candle to the pure genius and inventiveness of the original.

Carlos had tired of the wait and see attitude of the W.D.C. directors' staff. He felt that if anything would be done to stop the impending domination or destruction of the human race by the alien invaders, he would have to do it himself. Carlos secretly organized the small tight knit group of clandestine technicians and soldiers, hand picking each one for their abilities and loyalty to his cause. All of the cell members, having top secret clearance, were able to procure the equipment and personnel necessary to build a first strike weapon theoretically potent enough to bring one of Their ships down, hopefully without destroying it. They all knew that the great thing about government contracts and supply agreements lay in the system itself. All of the equipment and parts needed to assemble the weapon came from unrelated sources, making them untraceable. The only thing that the suppliers knew was that they had sold their own special part. They had no idea what the parts could be assembled into, and they didn't care. The complacency and greed of modern society was sure to be its undoing, but, for those that needed to get secret, dangerous things done, it was very convenient.

Make no mistake; to the last man, the cell members were in full agreement that, although there was a chance of starting a war, they believed that war was inevitable anyway. At least by making a first strike, the aliens would get a strong message from the inhabitants of Planet Earth - "Don't tread on me!"

What would the spineless bureaucrats in Washington and the foot draggers in the W.D.C. have to say about this course of action? Frankly, they didn't care, because they knew that it was the right thing to do, the only thing to do, if humans were to survive.

The main question concerning the aliens was, "Why were They holding out on us?" Some say that too much knowledge too fast could throw society into chaos, and that They only have our good in mind by promising to share their technology as the human race matures. Carlos fully understood that there were people in this world that would never understand what they had to do and why they had to do it. Carlos and the splinter cell that he organized and headed knew "the truth." They were poised for world domination. The only reason that They would come here was for living space or worse, a food source.

No matter what his personal sacrifices, he knew his duty, and, in his mind, this course of action was the only way to save mankind as a species. He also knew full well that there were others that would stop at nothing to keep him from his goal of bringing down an alien craft, exposing the government cover up, and, most importantly, taking possession of the medical and propulsion technology that had been denied the world.

***

Dreamland

Still surrounded by darkness, the 35-year-old Barry realized that he was safe and sound in his bed at the family compound. The experience had left him soaked in sweat and nearly hyperventilated. Lying there on the soggy sheets of his bed trying to relax and catch his breath, he pushed the apparent nightmare out of his mind. Barry was still trying to regain his composure when suddenly a familiar sound pierced the silence. Instinctively reacting, Barry immediately sprang from his bed. He hastily ran to the awaiting shuttle that ran down the south tunnel to one of four escape pods and quickly jumped in. Hurriedly pressing the big red control button labeled "forward," he couldn't believe it when nothing happened. "Dead! Impossible!" Franticly scrambling out of the escape shuttle, he started running the half mile down the tracks away from the screeching alarms and flashing lights. Barry's mind was racing. Could this be the real thing or just another exercise, just like all the other invasion scenarios that he and Sergeant Bill had constantly prepared for over the last several years?

"Intruder! North bunker!—Intruder! North bunker!"

In between the pulsing alarms and computer generated intruder announcements, he could hear the sound of running footsteps somewhere ahead of him just out of sight. The tunnel had filled with smoke by the time he arrived at the south bunker escape pod. Barry stumbled to a stop, and there, to his horror, lying on the floor in front of him, was Sergeant Bill. A shadowy figure stood over him, holding a weapon of some sort. Suddenly, the weapon emitted a bright light and buzzing sound.

"Taser!!!"

Then everything went dark.

***

Otis couldn't believe what he was seeing. They were slowly landing. As each of the ships slowly touched down, it was quickly surrounded by military troops. He could tell that the soldiers were just as excited, confused, and frightened as he was. The spacecraft now resting on the Capital lawn looked nothing like anything that could have been designed by the human mind. To many in the news room and on social media it appeared to be shaped like some sort of gigantic silk worm cocoon. The outer shell was constructed of some sort of seamless, black, luminescent material that glittered in the news media's flood lights. As the world watched in awe, the craft began to change from shiny black to flat black then began pulsating in a myriad of colors and shades of colors leaving the soldiers in a near hypnotic state. Not only was the color of the ship changing, but the shape of the ship itself was changing. The more time that passed, the more the ship changed. The new appearance of the craft had a predatory feel to it, looking for all the world like an Egyptian scarab beetle.

The ship/beetle rose from the grass on what appeared to be legs protruding from somewhere on its underbelly. Then, as if on command, the circle of media reporters and military spread out, leaving an opening in the parameter. The alien "bug" slowly crept across the capital lawn and came to a stop at the bottom of the main patio steps directly in front of a delegation of high ranking government officials. Otis was mesmerized by the proceedings transpiring on his plasma screen, but the more he thought about it, everything seemed just too familiar, as if the media had been trying to prepare the world for this moment by inundating the popular culture for untold years with stories and movies on the subject of outer space invaders. He then observed that within himself, he just wasn't that surprised.

***

Back in the bunker

Snow was beginning to fall and, as the wind picked up velocity, the ice on the aging power lines caused the lights to flicker in the remote research facility. Sylvia hoped that the power wouldn't go off again. She hated the dark. Something deep in her psyche abhorred the silence even though she claimed to love the solitude. It was foolish for a grown woman to be afraid of the dark. Afraid of the dark; there, she admitted it to herself.

The physical darkness itself wasn't the real problem. It was the feelings of separation and loss that always came rushing in that she feared. The anger that welled up inside her mind was, at times, unbearable. Sylvia preferred to work. At least with work, she could filter out the rest of the world, including the feelings about "Him."

Ultimately, Sylvia had lost Him during a power outage. Maybe that is why she hated the darkness so much. "He," being her long lost father Roy, was there for a couple of days physically after the blackout, but he was mentally disconnected. And then he was gone. Why did he leave her? Where did he go? She was only a child at the time. How could he leave her? How could he leave them all?

***

After the young Smith family's move to California, Sylvia's love of learning and studying minute details blossomed. Her academic life was nurtured early on by an astounding group of school counselors and mentors, one after the other, all gently guiding her toward one specific vocation - cartography, the study of maps and map making. Upon graduating high school a year early, Sylvia received a full ride scholarship to

Cal Polly on a newly instituted scholarship program funded by the United States Air Force. After university and graduate school, getting into the cartography program for N.A.S.A. was a dream, come true. Sylvia felt as if she was living a charmed life, as if someone was watching out for her and her family. Even now, when she looked back over her life, she could sense that somehow everything that happened was orchestrated. It was too much to just be a coincidence.

***

The storm seemed to be moderating, and the power had stabilized. Sylvia was glad once again for the solitude and lights. Now, she could concentrate on the G.P.S. readouts from her mainframe computer monitor. Although the computers had several hours of backup power, the satellite array and tracking systems relied on power supplied from the generator shack, so all she could do is work offline in the event that the power lines went down. There was still a lot of mapping to do on this old Earth, and she was elated to be part of the select few that were chosen by N.A.S.A for the ongoing task. Even with modern methods of cartography, only a small portion of the Earth's surface has been accurately documented and even less of the ocean floor. There was more information available to be documented and stored than could be gathered in a lifetime, but Sylvia had dedicated herself to do just that. She didn't just endure the isolation and the tedium, she relished in it.

***

Heroes or Murderers?

"Men, the time table has changed! We have less than twenty four hours to possible intercept. My source tells me that They will be passing over Devil's Tower sometime tomorrow night. We need to get the computer drives installed and get the "Bird" loaded. I know that we need time for testing the systems, but there just isn't time. All we can do is our best!"

Within an hour, Nikola had the hard drives installed, booted up, and running. The lack of glitches was surprising, and the whole team took it as a sign that they were doing the right thing.

Thirty-one feet long with a fully deployed wingspan of 28 feet, the Bird was a combination aerial drone/cruise missile, specially designed to fly at minimal airspeed for hours if need be, retract its wings, then accelerate to supersonic on demand. Although the drone was originally designed for runway takeoff, it had been modified for vertical launch by the addition of rocket boosters that would be ejected after reaching altitude and velocity. On the Bird's belly was a clear, polycarbonate dome covering what resembled a radar dish with a large eye at its center. An identical two foot diameter dome on the nose of the small aircraft protected another large lens. There were no identifiable markings on the Bird's sleek fuselage technically making it an unidentified flying object and subject to being shot down, that is if anyone could catch it. It had a top speed of Mach 6. The entire outer skin was composed of a cutting edge radar absorbing material that was so classified that even Carlos didn't know what to call it. The whole project and its components were so secret that in the event that the Bird were to be captured intact or destroyed, it was very unlikely that its function or origin could be discovered.

The Bird didn't contain any explosives and was essentially a flying, fiber optics cable with a jet engine attached. The plan was fairly simple - discharge a high energy directed beam from a ground based chemical oxygen iodine laser (originally designed for President Ronald Regan's "Star Wars" program) and hit a spot no bigger than a dinner plate on a target moving at supersonic speeds, five or more miles up. Once the beam had entered the lens target on the bottom of the Bird, it instantly passed through the fiber optic cable and out the lens on the front, which directed it to its intended target, up to ninety miles away. Even if the Bird was spotted by the Bogy, the laser beam, traveling at the speed of light plus flying velocity, puts the contact point at 670,618,484 miles per hour, give or take a couple of thousand.

Carlos had been able to "procure" everything that was needed to build a scaled down version that was nearly as powerful as its Navy counterpart. Nikola, a computer genius and laser expert, with the help of Popeye, a Navy Seal highly trained in electronic weapons systems, had programmed the over 120 billion lines of code to make the Bird fly and hit its target. The calculations required to "reach out and touch" a Bogy that is flying at possibly the speed of light was mind boggling beyond comprehension. Shooting at such a target without a positive point of reference would be like trying to hit a speck of dust in a hurricane by ricocheting a light beam off the rear view mirror of a car jumping the Grand Canyon, using a pin light.

That is where John came into the plan. Unknown to the military, the government, and most of the W.D.C., John was the medical technician that secretly implanted a tracking device into Barry when he was eleven. Sergeant Bill had taken him to a remote canyon to practice some mountaineering and survival techniques when Barry slipped and broke his ankle. At the time, Sergeant Bill thought that it was a good idea to have the tracker installed and to have, what he thought, was the only receiver.

The trouble with secrets is that sometimes they aren't secrets at all. John, being part of the government approved staff responsible for Barry's medical care had been approached by Carlos and been persuaded to make a clone of the signal encryption and eventually became part of the W.D.C. At the time Carlos didn't know exactly what the signal data could eventually be used for; he just knew that some day it would be very important if They came back for Barry. What astounded John was the question of how Carlos was aware of the procedure at all. The whole affair was on a need to know basis, and in John's estimation, Carlos didn't need to know.

It had been many years since Barry had been implanted, and John may have forgotten, but, most likely, he just couldn't imagine that Carlos would put the boy at risk. To take the chance of destroying even one human life in this kind of a venture would be unthinkable; it would send the message to the aliens that we are no better than they are.

Carlos was the only one that knew where the tracking signal would be coming from and that Barry's life was in the balance. The rest of the men were told that a tracker had been somehow placed onboard one of the extraterrestrial's ships by an unknown operative at one of the contact points. As far as the little splinter cell members knew, their objective was totally honorable, and, if successful, the world would proclaim them as Heroes.

***

Safe, maybe

Barry was still in emotional turmoil when he awoke with a jolt. His mind was whirling as he attempted to collect his composure. Laying there on his back with sweat and tears running off of his face, Barry eventually came to the realization that he was safe and alone on the summit of good old Devil's Tower. It had all been a terrible dream.

He had been looking forward to a night of tranquility and sky watching until a thick cloud bank began rolling in from the west, obscuring the night sky. Barry had checked the weather before making his ascent, and the sky was supposed to be clear for the next week, but like Sergeant often said, "Weather men are just like doctors and mechanics, all they do is guess." Even with his array of high tech surveillance equipment, there had been no sightings this night. With nothing to do but wait until morning, Barry had decided get some sleep, a decision that he now regretted.

Over the years, Barry had spotted meteors, comets, ball lightning, satellites, space junk, balloons, missiles, aircraft of all sorts, the space shuttles, and several top secret hypersonic drones, but he hadn't yet spotted the true focus of his attention-the alien craft and the extraterrestrials that had borrowed him as a child.

Since his mother Jillian, passed away from a rare form of leukemia fifteen years earlier, and when they weren't locked down in their mountain fortress, Barry and his step father, Sergeant Bill, had been wandering around the world, training the unseen armies of the W.D.C. (a clandestine organization known only to the most elite, super secret, paramilitary groups around the globe, dedicated to the defense of the planet Earth and its population against Alien invaders, by any means necessary).

As long as Jillian was still alive, Barry and Bill had been able to contain their wandering spirit, but, with her passing, all bets were off. After all, as Bill would say, "A moving target is harder to hit!" Besides their work with the W.D.C. they were determined to find the beings that had left such a void in the younger man's psyche. Barry's step father, on the other hand, had a whole other set of reasons for finding them.

Even though Barry was just a child at the time, he remembered the event as though it was yesterday. The whole thing was too hard to explain to anyone other than his mother and stepfather. Besides, even if he did have anyone else to tell, they wouldn't believe him anyway.

The memories of his childhood drew him back to the tower every year, like clockwork, on the anniversary of the Visitation. This year would be no different, but, for some reason, maybe because they were passing "just too close" to pass up an opportunity to climb the tower or maybe it was just fate, Barry and Bill had decided to stop by a month earlier than usual. Barry wasn't exactly sure why he came back or what he was hoping to happen, but he came anyway. Deep down, in part, he hoped to prove his stepfather wrong about the little interstellar Visitors that he had briefly known all those years ago.

Sergeant Bill didn't mind making the trip to The Tower. It always brought back a flood of good memories. After all, if it wasn't for 'The invasion," as he called it, Jillian and Barry wouldn't have ever been in his life. The fact that Sergeant Bill's step brother, Wayne Kenny, director of the W.D.C., had changed the training schedule at the last moment (a normal occurrence for security reasons) allowing for the stopover, didn't even cross their radar as being noteworthy. Bill and Barry were delighted at the opportunity.

***

The main hatch on the front of the alien "bug ship" opened wide allowing what appeared to be a ramp to extend to the top of the Capital patio stairs. Otis thought to himself that it looked like a tongue sticking out of a huge gaping mouth. In just moments, two small silver grey beings about four feet tall with large black pupil-less eyes stepped out of the bug's mouth into the lights. Otis somehow knew in his heart that everything would be alright. After all, if he had been prepared for an invasion like this, then the rest of the world, including the military, had to be ready also. Maybe it wasn't an invasion at all; maybe it was just a friendly Visitation. Besides, how could a race of diminutive creatures like that be a threat to us?

Chapter 3
Loss

Frozen and locked down

Snow was beginning to fall again. Well, fall wasn't exactly the right term. Sometimes it came in so thick that visibility was zero and sometimes it seemed to fly strait up off the ground. A person would have to remember to keep their cuffs tucked into their boots or they would get subzero snow blown up their pant legs. As the wind picked up velocity, the ice on the power lines running from the generator shack caused the lights to flicker in the remote research facility on the northwestern coast of Alaska near the top of the Bering Sea.

commandskywatch@nasa.gov:

Sylvia Smith:
Request extraction from research facility Northern Light: family crisis stated code 04832u76.
Sylvia Smith, Research Director, Northern light.

selsmithskywatch@nasa.gov:

Permission granted: code 04832u76
Be advised: it may take a few days. The weather has the whole region socked in. All aircraft are grounded till further notice. We will be there as soon as we get a break in the weather.
David Hearldson, Adcom, Skywatch.

Sylvia pushed her fingers through her curly blond hair and rubbed her temples with her thumbs in a subconscious attempt to release stress. Her normally twinkling blue eyes were blood shot from lack of sleep and a nagging headache that she had been nursing for the last couple of days.

"If this keeps up, I'm never going to get out of here!"

The facility itself was what is termed as a hardened facility, excavated 50 feet into solid rock and built out of solid concrete reinforced with steel. It was designed to withstand a direct bomber attack, possibly even a nuclear attack. If need be, it could be locked down and no one or no "thing" could get in.

Sylvia was afraid of hardly anything but she kept both of the huge three foot thick blast doors at the entrances locked down anyway. The blast doors weighed in at around twenty thousand pounds each and were normally actuated by electric servos and motors, but in emergencies and power outages they could be opened from the inside by using a hydraulic hand pump system.

The facility could also be opened from the outside by actuating a key pad on the doors or a hand held remote but only if an acceptance code had been entered by a control officer on the inside. The danger was a glitch in the security design. If you were caught outside in a power outage, even though you had dotted your I's and crossed your T's, it was impossible to get in without restoring the power. You had better pray that the battery in the generator shack was charged up or you couldn't get in then either. The hard and fast rule was never, never, never, forget the remote!!! Especially when you were alone at the facility.

The complex of outbuildings and bunkers had been built during the cold war for use as a covert listening post. At the time that Sylvia was there it was being used by NASA in conjunction with The Global Geological Survey, a research organization instituted through The World Research Association that was funded by a group of anonymous international investors. Sylvia was never sure who was paying the rent and payroll and she didn't really care as long as she got to do her research.

The Northern Light facility site was chosen because of its proximity to a military communications satellite in synchronous orbit five miles overhead. The aging spy satellite was converted to telecommunications via a half billion dollar grant supplied by yet another shadow corporation called Green Space. It had been thought by those that are supposed to know that it was impossible to refit a satellite while in orbit, but somehow it was. The whole operation was strictly on a need to know basis.

The converted outpost, sitting on a rugged mountain plateau was near enough to the Alaskan mainland to have some amenities such as electricity (if the power lines didn't go down) and delivery of food and other necessities via a small air strip. That is, when aircraft could get through the ice and bad weather that prevailed most of the year. Even in the middle of the Arctic Summer, a dangerous storm system could brew up in the Gulf of Alaska and cause blizzard conditions and hurricane force winds. The storm had been building over the last month, and, under normal circumstances, Sylvia would simply ride out the storm in her mega tough hidey hole, but the email from Brad was a total game changer. But for now, all she could do was wait.

There was plenty of food and supplies and staying warm was never a problem in the bunker because there was a geothermal well sunk deep into the Earth that provided a constant source of heat. Geothermal was beyond cutting edge when the facility was built, but for some reason it had never been upgraded to generate electricity. This was something that Sylvia found odd and disappointing, because she hated nursemaiding the generators. The fact that the power lines were exposed to the weather made no sense ether. It was just like the army to put such expense on one thing and slap something else together with no sense of logic at all.

The generator shack, as they called it, was located about fifty feet from the operation facility's back door, even though it didn't resemble a shack at all. It was built underground. The added distance was not only to avoid fuel and exhaust fumes from entering the living quarters but also prevented mechanical vibrations and E.M.F. waves from interfering with the sensitive listening arrays and satellite uplinks.

Sylvia knew that there was plenty of fuel, enough to last for several months, so, if the facility were to lose power, it would have to be the power lines. She knew that if the primary generator failed, the backup would kick in immediately, and, beyond that, there was the auxiliary bank of batteries that could run the facility on emergency power for at least a week. In the nineties, the military "Eggheads," as Sylvia was fond of calling them, installed some large solar electric panels. The only problem was that there just wasn't enough sunlight to charge the batteries.

The lights flickered and went off for a few seconds. It had to be the power cables! If things got any worse, she would have to put on her cold weather gear and go out into the minus fifty degree blizzard. Sylvia would have to snap her safety tether harness to the guide wire that ran between the back door of the living quarters and the generator shack in order to bypass the main power lines and string out an emergency extension cord. During her training, she actually did ask the officer in charge why the power transmission lines weren't buried under ground. Sylvia was curtly told, "Young lady, you ask too many questions. Dismissed!" It just confirmed her suspicions. Their heads were as hard as the rock that the facility was blasted out of.

Sylvia had never performed an emergency power transfer alone, but she had been extensively trained in all of the emergency procedures for the outpost. But dragging a frozen, two hundred pound power cable 60 feet, in sub zero temperatures, by herself, in the dark, just wasn't something that she was interested in doing. Sylvia was trained to do everything alone, but that was the sacrifice she had to make to maintain the solitude she yearned for.

Sylvia knew that, even though she was safe from the weather and anything else that the Alaskan wilderness could throw at her; she would have to be careful in everything she did, because, in a real emergency, there would be little or no chance of rescue, not for days anyway! Outside, there were a hundred ways to die.

Directly in front of the outpost entrance, the airstrip lay precariously close to a cliff face, which plummeted 300 feet to the surface of the Bering Sea below. Only the most experienced bush pilot dare attempt a landing. The majority of the time the supplies were dropped onto the runway at low altitude. There couldn't be any mistakes with the drop or the package could be too dangerous to retrieve. Even in good weather, a miss could mean the loss of the supplies over the cliffs. If the payload dropped in the forest, not only could it take hours to days to pack everything back to the supply area in the outpost, but there was always the danger of being attacked by a bear or wolves or, even worse, humans. That is why there was always bear spray and firearms available, and Sylvia was an expert marksman with handguns and rifle. But, for all of the dangers and deficiencies of creature comforts, life at the top of the world had its moments. In the summer, which seemed to last about a week, a person could get outside and enjoy the brief sunlight, and on a rare clear day one could see the Alaskan tundra to the east, the Bering Sea to the south, and, to the west, a glimpse of the Aleutian island chain - or so they say. Sylvia was always too busy to go outside and look.

***

South Dakota 1950s

Darkness crept across the craggy outcroppings that jutted out of the forest. The ancient granite monoliths, standing guard over the wilderness, cast their shadows with ever lengthening fingers of blackness. Neal and his unofficially adopted brother and hunting partner, Jack, along with wilderness outfitter and guide, Terry, were setting up camp for the night after an exhausting day of hunting and horseback riding in one of the many scenic canyons running through the Black Hills of South Dakota. The day's hunt had been disappointing, (only in the fact that the big Mountain Lion they had been tracking for two days had slipped out of range again) if you could call an expedition of a lifetime disappointing! In actuality, the two friends were overjoyed to just have the opportunity for an adventure such as this. Coming from totally different career paths (Jack was the owner-operator of a very successful wholesale office supply company, and Neal fabricated stainless steel food processing equipment), they had become friends while attending the same church. Otherwise, the two men probably would have never met, let alone become hunting buddies. Neal, an unassuming 55 year old, had struggled for months before the trip, trying to lose weight and get into some kind of shape. He had lost 30 pounds before getting into the wilderness and 10 more in the first four days afterward. Jack, a born leader and the older of the two by a couple of years, on the other hand, was in much better physical shape. To help clear his mind and to work off stress, he was a runner and hiker. But to be honest, nothing can prepare a person for riggers of wilderness horseback riding and primitive camping.

Jack and Neal had a kind of inside joke between them. When one of them got bruised, wacked by a bush, stuck by thorns, got really sore while riding, fell off their horse, or anything else that you might encounter while being out of your safety bubble, the injured party would smile (if possible) and utter the words, "It would kill a normal man!"

When the logistics of the trip seemed to be nearly impossible, they would laugh and give their battle cry, "It would kill a normal man!"

Getting time off work at the same time had taken a lot of planning and strategizing over the course of the previous two years, but they both agreed that all of the trouble and expense was well worth it.

Over the last four days, they had seen buffalo, elk, mule deer, whitetail deer, antelope, jackrabbits, wolves, coyotes, mountain lions, and a plethora of game birds. Jack had taken a monster bull elk on the first day out, and, on the third day, Neal had taken an antelope buck and a mule deer buck. All three of the magnificent animals were packed back to the hunting lodge for taxidermy trophy mounting and meat processing by Jesse and George, two roughnecks employed by the hunting lodge for just that purpose. This particular day's end had brought the adventurers to a long established wilderness camp at the mouth of an extraordinarily beautiful canyon called Dead Mule. The encampment was something that could be the subject of one of those huge paintings that people hang over their sofas or on the wall of their man cave. The four one room rustic trapper's cabins, three sleepers, and one cook house, built in the 1920s, were all constructed using natural pine logs cut from the forest near the camp itself. Small but comfortable in a storm, the cabins could accommodate up to four people each. There was no running water or electricity available, but the patrons didn't care; they actually preferred it that way. Plans had been discussed in the past to possibly put a water wheel and generator on the small stream that ran to one side of the camp, but it was tabled because there wasn't enough interest by the visitors in having such luxuries in the wilderness. Although there was much agreement and appreciation for the one communal privy that lay down a path into the woods

"Hey, Terry, why is this place called Dead Mule?"

"Well, boys, the legend went that a prospector in the 1870s lost his pack mule on the mesa during a thunderstorm, and the terrified animal ran blindly over the edge of the canyon to its death. Upon climbing down into the treacherous chasm and locating the mutilated mule and not having anything else to eat, the prospector drug the dead animal to the mouth of the canyon, made camp, and feasted on the mule for almost the whole winter."

With no dead mule available that night, the small hunting party would be enjoying a meal made from one of the most dangerous animals on the Great Plains, jackrabbit. Jack had dispatched the "Monster Jack" on the run with his .45 Colt cowboy revolver. Terry couldn't help but get in on the fun. He wheeled his horse Gambler around and yelled, "Good shot, Jack. It would have killed a normal man!"

For safety's sake, Terry had warned the men several times a day about the possibility of being thrown from their horses, on the occasion that a jackrabbit bolted out of the sagebrush at their horse's feet. Over the years, several people had been seriously injured, and one poor soul nearly died after being dragged by his horse. The interesting thing about the horses (especially Terry's personal horse, Gambler) trained by the wilderness outfitters was that they were unspookable under nearly any condition - thunder, lightning, birds, cars on the road, even shooting a firearm from or across the saddle; but there was just something about a jackrabbit that unnerved the beasts. Gambler, a fifteen year old, sixteen hand high Stud, was steadier than most due to Terry working with him daily, while most of the other horses were only on the trail seasonally. The old red horse was Terry's best friend, and the two were a perfect fit for each other. They were more than horse and master; it seemed at times that they could read each other's minds. Terry acquired Gambler when he was a two year old, taught him to saddle, and, over the years, rode him for over ten thousand miles. If Terry ever lost Gambler, he would be losing a large chunk of his life.

As Terry was putting the huge jackrabbit on the rotisserie rod over the campfire, he began to chuckle.

"Gentlemen, here's one that won't kill you!"

Jack walked over to the pack mule and rubbed its ears.

"I guess you're safe for another night, old buddy."

The smoke from the fire rising into the starlit cloudless sky, a cool breeze wafting the pungent bouquet of the lowland pines that cradled the campsite, the aroma of the food cooking over the crackling embers, and the company of good friends, Neal and Jack agreed it just didn't get any better than that.

The "Mountain Men," as they sometimes jokingly called themselves, were beginning to relax in the warmth of the roaring campfire and enjoy the jackrabbit and fried potatoes that Terry had expertly prepared when Neal chuckled and then asked the old trail guide a question.

"What was the biggest whitetail buck that you ever shot, Terry?"

"Well! Without bragging too much, did you see that eight by eight hanging on the lodge wall next to the kitchen?"

"That is for sure a good one, but did you ever kill one with your bare hands?"

Jack groaned slightly and buried his face in his hands.

"One day, a couple of years ago, Jack and I were heading home after three disappointing days of deer hunting on the Glade Top Trail system in the Ozarks, just north of the Arkansas border in Missouri. It was getting dark, so we were taking our time driving across a ridgeline gravel road called

Skyline Drive. Well, we came around this one corner; and there he stood, right in the middle of the road, the biggest buck that I had ever seen. I slowed the truck to a stop, and Jack quietly slid out the passenger door."

Jack groaned again.

"That big old buck just stood there; it must have been stunned by the headlights. Jack fired a round, and the buck jumped from the middle of the road and crashed through the cedars on the downhill side of the road. We knew that he was hit by the blood trail leading down the steep slope toward Chigger Gulch, an abandoned farm place. By that time it was getting real dark, so we pulled the truck off to the side of the road, grabbed a flashlight, and started tracking him. We lost the trail after about a hundred yards and were about to give up and come back in the morning. Then out of the corner of my eye, I saw a patch of white lying under a low cedar branch. We figured that he was dead, but I didn't want to take any chances so I pulled my hunting knife, grabbed his antlers, and proceeded to cut the buck's throat. Wouldn't you know it; that old buck jumped up with me on his back and started dragging me down through the boonies. After about 50 yards, I was able to get him killed. Well, we got him field dressed and started dragging the old buck back up the hill, and that is when we found the 10-pointer that Jack shot!!!"

All three of them started laughing, and almost in unison all three men blurted out, "It would have killed a normal man!!!"

***

1950ish Alaska

Wayne Kenny was the only person, other than Jillian and Barry that Sergeant Bill trusted completely. They had grown up together in a small frontier town located two hundred miles northeast of Anchorage, Alaska. Billy, as Wayne called him as a child was nearly killed when his parent's small airplane crashed during a freak thunderstorm over the Black Hills of South Dakota. It had taken nearly seven days before search crews found the wreckage. Billy's father Bill Taylor Senior had died instantly but despite her injuries his mother Melissa was able to cling on to life and to baby Billy. Luckily, the small airplane had gone down in a canyon near a stream. Although she had a broken back and broken legs, Billy's mother Melissa was able to drag herself to the stream and back. The pure mountain stream water gave them the life-sustaining moisture that they both desperately needed. Mother Melissa and baby Billy had stayed in the shelter of the overturned airplane with her dead husband's lifeless body still hanging upside down from the pilot's seat's safety harness for as long as she felt that they safely could.

Anguishing in pain from her injuries, she searched the cockpit again. Three days earlier she had found a small stash of snacks under the passenger seat. Maybe there would be something that she had missed. Melissa dragged her broken body up onto her knees. Writhing in pain, she began groping anxiously under the seats again. To her surprise, she found a box containing a flare gun and three flares clipped to the bottom of one of the seats. Melissa didn't know if their plane had even been missed, but she had great hopes that someone would see the flares and come rescue them. Struggling to get out of the broken airplane, she accidently fired one of the flares into the stream. Her heart sank, she had to be more careful or they would both die there in the wilderness.

Melissa listened intently for the sound of possible search planes. Hearing nothing but the wind in the pines and the babbling of the canyon stream, exhaustion and pain overtook her and she fell fast asleep. When she woke up, the moon was high in the star-studded night sky. Baby Billy was crying from hunger and fear so, after seeing to his needs, Melissa decided to fire another flare but this time she would be sure to point it skyward. Forcing herself to roll over on her back she clinched the flair gun in her remaining uninjured hand and squeezed the trigger. Nothing happened. Melissa dropped her arm to her chest in disbelief and exhaustion. Her mind was racing. Was the flair gun broken? Was it a faulty flair? Or was the safety on? Melissa laughed out loud as she remembered the premature launching of the first flair and how she had made sure to put the safety on. She once again mustered the energy to point the flair gun skyward, this time releasing the safety. The brilliant red glow of the flair streaked upward into the night sky momentarily illuminating the canyon walls and inadvertently driving away the hungry mountain lion that had been watching them from its vantage point on the rim of the canyon. Melissa watched and waited, hoping throughout the night that somehow someone had seen her distress signal.

With no food for seven days except for a few packages of snack crackers and with her husband's body decaying in the front of the plane, she made the desperate decision to use the last of the three emergency flares. Melissa was desperate, and desperate times call for desperate measures. She said her goodbyes to her dead husband, dragged her battered body and baby Billy as far away from the crash site as possible. After taking careful aim, she put the last flare directly into the open door of the airplane's cockpit. Melissa was fully aware that if no one saw the smoke and flames from the burning airplane then all would be lost, but that was just a gamble she would just have to make. The young mother watched as the flair sputtered and went out. She dropped her head in utter soul wrenching disappointment. That flair was her last chance to save her baby and herself. Melissa was sobbing in total despair when she heard a slight sizzling sound. She opened her eyes to see a small fire burning in the cockpit of the mutilated airplane. Soon the sizzling turned to popping then to puffing as the fire gained momentum. A plume of black smoke began rising up and out of the canyon, but would it be enough? Despair quickly turned to terror as she remembered that there were still 20 or 30 gallons of highly flammable aviation fuel in the wing tanks. Melissa franticly looked around. Was she far enough away from the impending explosion and fire ball? She cradled baby Billy under one arm and dragged her broken body to the edge of the stream with the other. Melissa didn't know how far the inferno would reach but, if she had to, she had decided to roll into the water with Billy underneath her. Within minutes the heat from the burning aircraft interior caused the fuel in the wing tanks to boil and expand. The pressure in the tanks soon became excessive, causing the filler caps to blow off. As soon as the hot vaporized fuel reached the air and flame, it detonated. The ensuing explosion threw the burning airplane into the air like a child's toy. Melissa was frozen with fear as the heat and pressure wave passed just over their position leaving her and baby Billy unscathed. Melissa looked up just in time to see the crumpled hulk of the little airplane fall back to the bottom of the canyon some 40 feet away. The heat in the canyon had increased dramatically making it nearly unbearable. Melissa slid into the stream, making sure to hold her child's face up so he could breath. The fuel driven fire ball quickly dissipated allowing the temperature to plummet. Melissa franticly checked to see if her crying child had been injured. When she felt the fire (that was now raging farther up the canyon walls) was no longer an extreme danger, she crawled out of the water (baby Billy in tow) and collapsed against a log on the side of the stream.

***

On the range again

The three "Mountain Men" were still laughing when they heard a deep rumbling sound that seemed to be coming from somewhere up the canyon.

"Did you hear that, Terry?"

"Yes, sir, I did!"

"What do you make of it?"

"I don't think it was thunder!"

"It can't be thunder. The weather reports said all clear for almost all of the state!"

Terry had already jumped to his feet and was intently looking and listening in the direction of the rumble.

"Well, just to be sure, I better call the lodge!"

Fortunately for Terry, he hadn't yet taken the saddles off of the horses or unloaded the pack mule that, among other things, was carrying a military surplus two-way radio. He quickly opened the watertight wooden box (labeled **DYNOMITE** just for effect) that was attached to the pack saddle on the mule and removed the radio from its safety case. After opening the back of the unit to make sure that none of the vacuum tubes were loose or broken, Terry turned the then state of the art WWII surplus Walkie-Talkie on to warm up. After extending the collapsible antenna and turning up the volume, the radio crackled and hissed as it came to life.

"Fire Station Six, this is Range Rider. Come in!"

Terry checked the meters on the front of the unit. He could tell that there wasn't any signal strength where he was. The range rider would have to go to higher ground.

"Fire Station Six, this is Range Rider. Come in!"

There was still no signal.

"Sorry, guys, the whole effect of being alone on the range in the pioneer days will just have to wait. I am going to have to get to higher ground for a signal. Enjoy your supper, I will be back soon."

The horses, the pack mule, and the cabins, everything was chosen to be as authentic as possible. Terry himself wore turn of the century styled cowboy boots, riveted jeans covered by leather chaps, a gun belt that cradled his father's old Colt Peacemaker, and a black and red plaid flannel shirt, accented by a blue bandana. The whole look was topped off by his salt and pepper beard and a raggedy, sweat stained, brown 10-gallon cowboy hat that he wore kind of lopsided on his wind-weathered brow. Terry's blue piercing eyes and easy going demeanor always exuded confidence, determination, and honesty. He was a man that you would want for a trusted friend.

Terry took his position as a wilderness guide very seriously. Although the real impetus of the trail rides was realism, safety was of upmost importance. He removed the radio and a large bulky flashlight from the storage box on the pack mule. Terry slipped the Walkie Talkie over his shoulders, securing it on his back, turned on the flashlight, then mounted old Gambler, and began heading up to the rim of the canyon. Once on top, and after getting a signal, Terry tried calling again.

"Fire Station Six, this is Range Rider. Come in!"

"Fire Station Six, this is Range Rider. Come in!"

"Range Rider, this is Fire Station Six. What can I do for you, Terry?"

"We heard a big explosion or something about twenty minutes ago, Angie, so I came up on the ridge to see what I could see. There is a fire approximately two miles north east of our location in the bottom of Dead Mule Canyon. The fire doesn't seem to be natural. The color is very unusual, and the smoke is black like it is from some kind of fuel! Do you want us to investigate?"

"It might be the airplane that went missing last week. The Army and the Boy Scouts have been searching high and low for days now with no luck. If it is the airplane, the chances of it exploding on its own after all this time are slim to none. Someone or something had to set it off. I am going to dispatch a chopper from fire rescue now, but go ahead and work your way up the canyon. It will take the chopper an hour or two to get there from Fire Base Twelve. The ground rescue crews are three canyons to the east and at least eight hours away. Someone may need help before the chopper team gets there! Be careful!"

"Will do, Sis! Range Rider out!"

It was totally dark by the time Terry, the wilderness guide, rode back into camp. The skies were clear, and all three of the men could see a red glow in the sky and hear a slight rumbling sound farther up the canyon.

"Something's seriously wrong. Would you guys mind coming with me? I may need all the help I can get! And, I have to be honest; it could kill a normal man. We may be looking for a downed airplane, and there might be lives on the line."

Neal and Jack could tell by the serious tone of Terry's voice that the situation was dire or else they would not have been asked to be involved in the search. The two friends both agreed that the circumstances had changed, and, after all, one adventure was as good as another. Besides, it would fall under the precept of doing the right thing simply because it is the right thing to do. The willingness to "go with the flow" and adapt to changing circumstances was one of the many things that had drawn the two friends to each other.

"Lead on, Boss!"

Neal and Jack each took a flashlight from Terry, then quickly mounted their horses, before cautiously following him up a winding trail to the top of the canyon rim. Far off in the distance, they could see a plume of black smoke rising from a huge ball of fire as sparks from the sagebrush burning along the sides of the canyon wall twinkled in the night sky like millions of fireflies. The sight was both beautiful and terrifying.

It had taken the better part of an hour to get to a vantage point at the top of the canyon above the fire, after picking their way by flashlight through the brambles and bushes along the edge of pending disaster in the darkness. Coming to a stop, Terry smoothly slid his six foot frame from Gambler's saddle, patted the old horse on the back of his head, and then retrieved the Walkie-Talkie from its place on his back. After expertly hooking the straps of the radio backpack over the saddle horn, he once again opened the back of the unit and rechecked the vacuum tubes before turning the power switch to the on position. Terry noted the signal meter and then keyed the microphone.

"Fire Station six, this is Range Rider. Come in!"

"Range Rider, what is your position now?"

"We are on the rim of the canyon about a hundred yards from the site and are getting ready to make our descent. We couldn't reach the position directly above the fire. There is just too much smoke and heat. I think that there will be less smoke at the bottom."

"Be careful, Terry. We don't want to have to rescue you three yahoos too."

Neal looked at Jack with a look that said he felt that this really could kill a normal man. After retrieving the Walkie Talkie, a first aid kit, a 150 foot long length of rope, and some basic food and water supplies, the three men left their horses and the pack mule tied to a tree, then started working their way down from the rim of the canyon on foot. The climb down through the loose gravel and sage brush was treacherous, and by the time they reached the bottom of the canyon they were all scraped up and exhausted. After rechecking his equipment, Terry tried the radio. Much to his delight, it crackled then beeped. The signal was weak but workable. A faint, scratchy voice called to him from across the miles.

"Range Rider, this is Fire Station six. What is your status?"

"We are in the bottom of the canyon, about a hundred yards from the site. The fire is still burning farther up the canyon, but seems to be losing intensity, although the sagebrush on both sides is still fully involved."

"Be advised, the fire rescue chopper is still 20 minutes out. Be careful, Terry. If the wind changes direction in the canyon, you could be facing an inferno!"

"Thanks, Angie. If the tables turn, we will shelter in the creek. Hold on! Did you guys hear that? What the heck! Is that a baby crying? I'll have to get back to you, Sis! Rider out"

"Terry!!! Terry!!! Come back, Terry!!!"

The three men redoubled their efforts in clawing their way up the canyon toward the cries. Scrambling to within a hundred feet of the fire, another voice, almost too faint to hear caught their attention. Curled up against a log, Melissa and baby Billy, dirty, beat up, and starving, but still alive, both cried out - baby Billy because of exposure and the worst case of diaper rash in the history of the world and Mother Melissa just out of pure joy.

"Hold on, Terry, do you see that?"

***

Otis watched intently as the media circus of the millennium swelled to a frenzied pace, with the whole world watching on. Every eye was on "the greatest event in the history of the world," or so the television moderators were calling it. The whole world was pulsing in a party-like atmosphere, in anticipation of great things to come.

***

On the island

The satellite phone hissed and crackled as the signal made its way through the atmosphere, leaving the connection weak and tentative at best.

Toby ran to his A.T.V. and grabbed the satellite phone from its latch on the handlebars. Quickly glancing at the phone's display, he softly chuckled.

"Big Joe's Bar B Q! You choke it, we'll smoke it! How can we help you?"

"Oh! Grow up, Toby!"

"What's up, Sis?"

"You need to be getting out of there. The eye in the sky says that your friendly little mountain has grown nearly two inches over the last 24 hours. I'm not a big bad volcanologist like my big brother, but my gut says that it is about to blow!!!"

"You worry too much, Sylvia! Sure, we're getting some movement, but this one shows all the signs of being a puffer. The team members here and the Global Geological brain trust on the mainland all agree that if it erupts at all, it will be unimpressive at best.

"Maybe so, but I still wish that you would catch the next steamer to the coast!'

"It's not like you to be upset like this! Is something else going on? Is Mom alright?"

"Brad sent an Email that didn't sound very good. Apparently Mom is beginning to hallucinate now, along with her heart problems."

"Hallucinations!   What on Earth is she hallucinating about?"

"You're not going to believe it!!!! Him! The old man! She thinks that he has been coming to see her at night. Toby, you need to come home now!! I'm trying to get extracted as soon as the weather breaks. I hope it will be soon enough. I have a bad feeling about this, Brother; we may lose her this time."

"Whoa!! Take it easy!! I will try to call the supply boat back tomorrow. I can be there in a week if all goes well."

"Please hurry, Toby!"

"I will!! I will!!!"

The satellite phone crackled again, and the signal was gone.

***

Deadeye

The baby's cries had not gone unnoticed by the large male mountain lion silently creeping through the darkness. The hungry cat had braved the flames and smoke of the canyon walls, arriving at the crash site moments before Terry, Jack, and Neal drawn to the smell of decaying flesh and the pitiful cries of baby Billy. The big cat was slowly maneuvering around the front of the downed airplane when Neal spotted it.

"Holy cow, there it is!"

Just as the hungry predator leaped toward Melissa and baby Billy, Jack fired one round from his trusty Colt .45 dropping the killer animal in a heap just a couple of feet from its intended target. He fired two more rounds "just to make sure."

The three men quickly made their way to Melissa and baby Billy's side. After making sure it was dead, Jack and Neal drug the mountain lion away from the injured plane crash victims, as Terry quickly tried to evaluate their condition.

Terry keyed the microphone on the radio.

"We have them! Repeat! We have them!!"

"You have who, Terry?"

"I don't know, but two out of the three are alive! It was an airplane! I mean it is an airplane or at least what is left of an airplane! How the mother and baby survived I will never know! They are badly injured and really weak. When will that chopper be here?"

"You should be hearing it very soon! Did you say a mother and baby?"

The three "Angels," as Melissa called them, gave baby Billy and her the food and water they had carried down into the canyon, then stayed close by their side until they were safely lifted out of danger by the rescue chopper crew. After the young mother and child were safely deposited at the nearest hospital, the helicopter returned and, as a favor to Terry, pulled all three men and the dead mountain lion out of Dead Mule Canyon.

The sun was coming up over the South Dakota plains as the weary "Angels" finally rode back into camp. Jack looked at his friend, Neal, and then at Terry, with a grin on his face.

"Well, Boss, we got that mountain lion, so what's next?"

***

When the nurses entered the room, Brad was standing by his mother's side.

"Roy!! Roy!! Where are you?"

"I don't know, Mom."

"How are you doing, Hun?"

"Where are you, Roy?"

"Calm down, Miss Smith. Your heart won't take very much of this."

"Everything's alright, Mom! You're alright! I'm right here!"

Brad was on the verge of crying when a second nurse came in with a hypodermic needle, uncapped it, proceeded to purge it of air, and then injected medication into the I.V. port attached to the drip line in Ronnie's arm. While the sedative went to work and the good memories began to overshadow the bad memories, Ronnie's stress levels began to diminish, which was reflected on her heart monitors.

"Is she going to be alright nurse?"

"That is yet to be seen. Do you know why she got so agitated?"

"No, Ma'am. She was just waking up, and all of a sudden she started calling out for my father."

"Where is your father? Can I call him for you?"

"No, Ma'am, my father is dead."

***

Three months before Roy's homecoming
20 miles from the hospital

"Good morning, Gus! How's it going?"

Bill Adams was Gus's immediate supervisor and a work place friend. Gus looked up from his computer monitors with a startled, almost terrified, look on his face.

"Are you alright, Gus? We are getting worried about you!"

"I knew that they would come for me, but I didn't think it would be you!"

"What are you talking about, Gus? Who is coming for you?

"The ones that took away all the others!!!! And now they've turned you against me!!!! Haven't I been working hard enough? Why are they watching me? There are cameras in the light fixtures and monitors you know!!!! I can hear them talking through the walls!!!!"

"Gus, you're obviously having a little problem. As a friend, let me call the company doctor to come check on you."

"Don't listen to him, Gus. He can't be trusted. He will have you killed like the others."

"No!! No!!! No!!!! I won't go, and you can't make me. I will fight them!!!!! I will fight them all!!!!!!! I know what happened to the others!!!!!!! I heard their screams as they were being dragged away to the death camps!!!!!!!!"

"Run while you can, Gus!!!! They're coming!!!!!! Run!!!!!!!!!!!!!

Gus was a young man of 25 when he married his high school sweetheart Margaret, or Maggie as he lovingly called her. The young couple had been very happy in their little town house located in a small bedroom community on the coast. After Gus graduated from college with a master's degree in computer science and Maggie completed nurse's training, they had been looking forward to living a "normal" life. Seeming to have it all, Gus and Maggie were a typical young urban professional, or "yuppie," couple with all of the "normal" dreams and aspirations. Gus was a body builder on the amateur circuit with hopes of going pro at the end of the next season or so, but, to make a living, he had secured a prestigious position as a lead systems analyst for a huge multinational financial group located nearly 40 miles away from home in the heart of "the city". They felt at the time that their life together was going so well; they were making plans to start a family.

All had been going very well for the young couple until the national economy tanked. Gus's department was a victim of downsizing, and he had lost most of the personnel in his department. As with most white collar jobs, less workers only meant that the remaining "drones" had to pick up the slack and the pressure to perform increased exponentially. He was practically living at the office when the voices began to speak to his subconscious; quietly at first then slowly growing in intensity. Within a week he was beginning to see things and people that weren't there. As the paranoia increased, Gus became suspicious of everyone around him, even his beloved Maggie.

Inside the protective walls of his office, he could function well, or so he thought. Gus was changing. As the days progressed, reality began slipping away. He started forgetting to go home, to eat, to change clothes, and bathe. Gus's boss remembered the day that he came to check on his well being, at the behest of his wife Maggie and his coworkers.

Finding him dirty, disheveled, and confused, he had offered to try and get Gus medical help, but he would have none of it. Then later in the day, Gus forgot where he was, where he worked, and, worst of all, he forgot Maggie.

Maggie waited patiently for the love of her life to call or come home from work in "the city." It had been nearly a week since she had seen him. It wasn't totally unusual for him to be out of touch because of the demands of his job, but he usually would call her at least once a day. It had been three days with no contact when she got an urgent call from Gus's boss.

"Margaret! This is Bill, Gus's supervisor! I was really covered up when you called and insisted that I check on him. I am really sorry that I didn't go sooner. We are really concerned about him."

"What's wrong?"

"Apparently he has been acting very strangely all week long, and now he is gone."

"Gone, what do you mean gone?"

"Well ... I went in to check on him like you asked, and I didn't like what I found. I tried to offer him some help, and he went berserk. He started accusing me of trying to get him fired, to undermine his efforts, all sorts of outrageous things. Margaret, Gus accused me of plotting to have him killed! Then he grabbed his head and started yelling "No! No! No!" as he ran down the hall and out of the building. I tried to stop him, but he was too strong! He tossed me out of his way like I was a rag doll."

"Do you know where he is now?"

"No, we can't find him. We all searched the building and grounds for him; he seemed to just disappear. Margaret, we have called the Police, and they are looking for him now. Margret, I want you to know that I only called the police so he could get some help. I'm so sorry! I should have seen something happening. Maybe we could have... maybe.... I hope they can find him. He's like a member of the family. Tell him when you find him that he is very much welcome to come back to work when he can."

Maggie immediately decided to take leave from her nursing job at the emergency clinic, where she had worked since graduating last spring, and drove the 40 odd miles to Gus's work place in the city.

***

Gus ran from building to building, making sure to stay clear of security cameras and guards. Every voice he heard, every person he met was a threat to his very life.

Run, Gus. Run or you're a dead man!!!!

He wasn't sure why they wanted him dead, but he wasn't about to stick around and find out. Gus quickly found his way to the storm drain system that ran along the backside of a nearby city park. The poorly maintained drainage ditch was nearly covered by bushes and small trees, giving Gus the cover that he desperately needed to escape his pursuers. Now, covered from head tom foot with mud and debris, Gus was all but invisible to the police officers that were by then searching the streets and byways, trying to bring him in for a welfare evaluation. The police officers were very well intentioned, but they were looking for a mildly disturbed man wearing a white shirt, blue tie and black dress pants; not a highly paranoid, extremely frightened individual that had more resemblance to a wild animal than a man.

Gus belly-crawled a couple of hundred yards down the muddy drainage ditch to where it joined a 30 feet wide, 10 feet deep, open-topped concrete culvert. He decided to wait for the cover of darkness before sliding out into the open.

They're looking for you. You had better keep out of sight!!!!

By nightfall Gus had begun to relax somewhat but, although his overwhelming fear had subsided a bit, his paranoia had not. A couple of hours after dark, he dropped the six feet out of his muddy refuge and cautiously began creeping down the flat bottom, open-topped culvert toward the gaping mouth of the underground storm drainage system some half mile away. The moon was shining brightly, causing Gus to work his way through the shadows on one side of the culvert. He would take a few steps, stop, and listen. Then when he felt that he could, he would take a few more. After a half hour of creeping, he was nearing the tunnel opening when he heard voices from the street above. Gus's fight or flight response instinctively kicked in, and he ran undetected into the darkness and safety of his new underground sanctuary.

Gus sat huddled in the darkness looking and listening for any movement or threat. The voices in his head were raging, and he was unable to concentrate on any form of plan or direction.

Go!!! Go!!! No, I'm tired!!! They all hate you!!! I know!!! The whole Earth hates you!!! I know!!! You need to keep on running!!! I have to be somewhere!!! Go!!! Go!!! Nobody will miss you anyway!!! Go!!! Go!!!

After two days and nights, the tumult slowed to a dull roar and he was finally able to doze off. His solitude was to be short lived. Unbeknownst to Gus, it was Sunday morning, and every Sunday morning for the past 30 years, a small group of Christians made the rounds handing out sandwiches, clothing, Bibles, and love. He woke with a start but remained frozen in silence. Gus believed that if he couldn't see them then they couldn't see him. He was right about the church group but his arrival in the "underbelly" had not gone unnoticed.

***

After days of searching with the police and by herself, driving relentlessly up and down every street and byway that was even remotely safe for her, Maggie finally came to the conclusion that, if she were to find her love, she would have to move there instead of sleeping in an unused storage room located in the basement of Gus's workplace. She soon found a small efficiency apartment as near as possible to the area where he was last seen. Maggie searched until her strength and funds had all but run out.

Even though she had a nursing degree, a full time job at the hospital across the street was out of the question, she needed every minute available to look for Gus. As luck would have it, she was able to get a part time night job as a waitress in a diner, close enough to walk to work. It would allow her to work nights and search the hospitals and streets in the daytime when it was less dangerous. The job also made it possible for her to meet many of the street people that frequented the small diner and the dumpsters around behind.

"Somebody out there had to know something!"

***

Wheels up, maybe

After finishing his meal and offering his pleasantries and tip to the beautiful young waitress, Brad went outside to get into his little yellow street rod. As he walked across the parking lot, he was glad that he had taken the time to pull on the form fitted, forest pattern camouflage, car cover. Apparently a flock of migrating birds had decided to take a break in the tree above his parking space. Luckily, the grounds man had been watering the shrubs, and Brad was able to quickly hose off the birds "contributions," once again making it look like a car shaped hedge instead of a small hill with snow on top. He didn't know if the camo cover fooled anyone, but it was less conspicuous than a bright yellow sports car.

After fluffing and stuffing the camouflage car cover, he thanked the grounds man as he rumbled his way out of the parking lot. On the short drive back to the sprawling Air Force base, many thoughts and concerns again filled his mind. It had been over a year since Sylvia had been home for even a short visit, and Toby had been gone for over three years. Sure, their work was important, but Mom needed them more now than ever. Brad would never admit it to them, but he needed them too.

Brad revved the engine of his shiny yellow road rocket as he waited to pull forward in the traffic line leading to the airbase gate. He loved the way that the little street rod rocked back and forth with the torque of the huge V-8 engine. The little but powerful racer was a kit-built replica of an A.C. Cobra. Sitting low to the ground, the pair of chrome plated side pipes hung just inches from pavement, and the chrome single roll bar behind the driver's seat set off the look of the mighty little machine.

A smartly dressed sentry at the gate, looking very professional in his crisply pressed light blue shirt and dark blue pants, greeted Brad with the usual "good evening, Colonel" and then put his hand out for his identification card. As the sentry turned to swipe his card, Brad took note of the chrome whistle clipped to his pocket, the semiautomatic side arm and radio attached to his belt, and the two fully automatic assault rifles standing at the ready between the sentry on his side of the gate booth and the sentry on the outgoing side. Although the sentries were employed by a civilian security company, they were highly trained, and the use of deadly force was authorized. In case of an intrusion, they would not hesitate to protect the base.

After clearing the security check point and driving under the slowly rising red and white striped barrier arm, two soldiers standing on the sidewalk recognized him and saluted. Returning the salute, he punched the throttle as he passed, which pleased the men very much.

Making his way across the half mile to hanger roe, Brad slid the roadster into his designated parking space causing the extra wide rear tires to "bark." He punched the accelerator once just to hear the engine's exhaust rumble and echo off the giant aircraft hangars. Soon Brad would be back doing his most favorite activity in the entire world. All he had left to do was have a short flight plan meeting with the four trainees under his tutelage and then "suit up." The young pilots, all four of which were classmates from the Air Force Academy at Colorado Springs, were all top notch flyers. Coming from very diverse social and ethnic backgrounds, they had found a way to overcome their differences and bond into a very tight knit team, almost too tight knit in Brad's opinion. He worried how the group would respond in a battle situation, especially if one of them went down. The flight plan meeting was short and concise. After reminding the trainees again of the pitfalls of complacency and the very real dangers of flying at supersonic speeds, Brad dismissed them with a salute.

"Suit up men and meet me on the tarmac in twenty. We go wheels up within the hour."

After taking a quick shower, he slipped into his special made, form fitted, pressurized flight suit and then headed for the hangers.

***

The underbelly

Pastor James and four of his outreach group had been in the "underbelly" for over an hour, cave lights on their heads, wagons full of supplies in tow; handing out acceptance and love.

"Good morning, Preacher. Sure is good to see you."

"Good to see you too, Noah. Are you doing alright?"

Pastor James had given the homeless man the nickname of Noah because several years back he survived being caught in one of the many yearly flashfloods and had nearly drowned.

"Doin' right well, preacher."

"Is there anything we can do for you, my friend?"

"Not today, but you might be able to help the newbie. Whoever it is came in a couple of days ago and is holed up about 500 feet from the mouth by north park."

"Do you think they are alright?"

"Yeah, I can hear em' breathin' and movin' around down there, but I bet their gittn' hungry though. I'll give em' the message if wanna leave a package at Heart Plaza."

"Do you think they're a man or a woman?"

"Man fer sure. Heard em' cough once."

"We will leave him some clothes too. Do you have any idea what size he might be?"

"Not for sure but he sound like a big un'."

"You have good ears and a good heart, my friend. God bless you, and we will see you next week."

Noah waited for about an hour before he tried to contact the "newbie" by shouting at the top of his lungs in the direction of the north park drainage tunnel entrance.

"If yer' hungry, go to the heart!!! There won't be no buddy there ta hurt cha!!!"

Gus was most definitely hungry, but it still took him several hours before he could muster up the courage to leave his hidey hole. He had been hearing something that sounded like a heartbeat ever since he entered the storm drainage system but hadn't paid any attention to it until Noah shouted to him.

Gus began following the sound of the beating heart while feeling his way along the side of the tunnel by dragging a stick against the concrete wall. The tunnels, for the most part, were totally dark except for vent openings to the surface that let in light. As he followed the heartbeat Gus occasionally encountered an intersection where it was hard to tell which way the sound was coming from (or unexplainably silent), but at each intersection there was a vent and in the light of the vent was a symbol of a heart with an arrow through it pointing the way. As Gus got closer, the heartbeat got louder and louder. He rounded a corner and entered a large chamber with several tunnels opening into it. In the center of the chamber ceiling was a large grate with sunlight flooding through it. On the floor of the chamber was a box containing food, bottled water, clothing, flashlight, and maps of the city (with all of the shelters highlighted) and of the storm drain system. On top of the box was a weatherproof Bible containing bus tokens and directions to the church and ultimately, to Heaven. Gus looked and listened intently before stepping into the chamber. The heartbeat stopped causing Gus to freeze in his tracks. After a few moments of terror, from the street above, a car horn sounded, an angry voice shouted something rude, and the heartbeat slowly resumed. In his compromised and confused state, he still laughed. It was cars running over a manhole cover! Gus took the box and headed back into the darkness where he sat for sometimes days at a time, venturing out only when he was on the brink of starvation.

In the days and weeks to come (when he was lucid that is), Gus would slowly and cautiously seek out places of safety and food, eventually coming across a diner that always had food available at least once a night and a vision of an angel that he called "the woman in white".

***

Exercise in futility

The sun was setting over the Pacific Ocean and an unusually beautiful cascade of color painted the evening sky, as the night operations Fighter wing crews were preparing for an integrated avionics system training flight led by Colonel Bradford R. Smith. The advances in avionics and fly by wire technology over the last decade had greatly increased the fly-ability and safety of military aircraft. Before the advent of the helmet mounted display, or H.M.D., most pilots, except for some privately licensed operators, had undergone instrument flight rules, or I.F.R., training and testing on an annual or semiannual basis.

Often referred to as flying under the hood, pilots were required to take off, maneuver, navigate, and land entirely by instruments. The training was, quite literally, under the hood. A flight helmet was fitted with a visor that made it impossible to see the horizon or the sky above, forcing the pilot to rely only on instrument readings. This training was essential for flying at night or in any environment that prevented good line of sight, such as in smoke or clouds. With the addition of the H.M.D. technology, the instrument panel and the cockpit became secondary when it came to navigation and targeting. Equipped with heads up displays for radar and infrared viewing on a 360 degree basis, these "Warbirds" could see in the dark, through clouds, smoke, or any other airborne obstruction, making them deadly under any circumstances and at any speed.

After suiting up, Brad tucked his flight helmet under his arm and walked out of the locker room toward the huge hanger door. On the way into the sunlight that was streaming into the hanger from the west, three soldiers dressed in Air force digital camouflage utility uniforms snapped to attention and saluted. After Brad returned the salute, the eldest of the three stepped silently forward and stood at ease.

"Is she fueled and run out, Chief?"

"Yes Sir, Colonel!"

"Any anomalies, Chief?"

"No, Sir, not on my watch, Sir! Sir, how is your mother, Sir?"

"Flying slow and level for now. Thanks for asking, Chief."

Brad scrambled up and over the wing, quickly settling into the cockpit of the magnificent twin engine war bird. Looking to his right and then back to his left; he could see the other four pilots gingerly mounting their aircraft. The look on their faces exuded the pride and pure ecstasy of the privilege that they were about to participate in.

Sitting silently on the ground, the aircraft looked as if it could jump into the sky at any moment. Brad never failed to be thrilled by the sheer gracefulness and raw power that the aircraft silently exhibited, not to mention that his name was smartly monogrammed on both sides just below the canopy. There could be no doubt who pilots this screaming sky sled - Colonel Bradford R. Smith. Since his acceptance to flight school, Brad had given much thought to a proper call sign that would be placed under his name and rank along the sides of his fighter. He had many ideas, most of which were names of birds of prey or man eating predators, something that would sound very warrior-like in a war zone.

Brad had been assigned under the best instructors and had graduated at the top of all his classes, but, for reasons that he couldn't understand, he had never been allowed out of the country, let alone into an actual combat zone. Brad had cautiously questioned his superiors several times about the situation and at every turn was shut down. After receiving a curiously worded "cease and desist" document directly from the Pentagon, he thought better of pushing it any farther, at least for then. Until that opportunity presented itself, Brad would have to be content with training the next generation of sky warriors. As much as he wanted a heroic sounding sign, he knew that, ultimately, it was an "honor" given to flyers by their peers for doing something stupid or unique. The call sign that Brad had been labeled with definitely wasn't what he would have chosen for himself, but, it could have been worse.

As Brad focused on the task at hand, he began to push his personal feelings and concerns to the back of his mind. He knew that a distracted pilot is a dead pilot. He couldn't do anyone any good if he wasn't alive to be there.

Brad chuckled to himself as he adjusted his lucky charm on the instrument panel. The three by five black and white photograph of a young woman was one of his most favorite possessions. Dressed in white shirt and tie, topped with a brown leather flight jacket and nicely fitting black slacks, the W.A.S.P. (Woman's Air Force Service Pilot) seemed to beckon to him from the past. She was standing just behind the wing of a shiny new P51 Mustang, her hair blowing in the airplane's prop wash. There was a look on her face that, for Brad, conjured up feelings of melancholy and wonder. He couldn't help but wonder what this beauty was thinking when the photo was taken and, for that matter, what happened to her. The whole story was deeply intriguing to him, much more than he would ever let anyone know.

A little innocent fanaticizing about a woman he had never met, and never would, was his way of relieving stress. By being in love with a ghost instead of a flesh and blood living person, he could avoid the normal encumbrances and inconveniences, besides the fact that being dead, she couldn't possibly abandon him. Making no mistake, Brad definitely preferred the company of women, but, for now, he didn't have time for a real woman. In the back of his mind though, he someday wanted to settle down and have "it all," including a wife, children, and a home of his own. Although the huge house that his mom had won in that mysterious raffle all of those years ago was the place he called home, Brad just didn't think that a Colonel in the Air Force should be living with his mommy after he got married. Next door would be alright though, providing that his mother survived long enough to see that day. Brad's alter ego, Colonel Bradford R. Smith, soon took over as he pulled his flight helmet into place and the "H.M.D." blinked into view. "The Colonel" was all business, by the book, one hundred percent gung ho.

"Tower, AF037, Infield One request engine start."

"Stand down, Colonel."

Brad sat there stunned for almost a minute.

"Say again, Tower!"

"Stand down, Colonel."

"Can I get an explanation, Tower?"

"Classified Sir, came down from high up."

"Thank you, Tower. AF037, Infield One, out."

Brad sat there in his cockpit contemplating his next move. It was disappointing, but orders were orders.

"Well, gentlemen, you heard the man. Deplane and have a good night off."

Although the situation was perplexing, such unexplained order changes was something that all military men had to get used to. Brad was exhausted, he knew that his mother was in good hands and a good night's sleep would do him good. Within an hour and a half, Brad was fast asleep in his recliner at the family home. He had only meant to sit and catch up on the daily news when his sleep deprivation over took him.

***

The first visit

Crunching his way across the chip and seal roof made him almost giggle. Roy had forgotten so many things over the decades that he had spent in space: the smell of the night air, the twinkle of the stars through Earth's oxygen rich atmosphere, and the bugs that seemed to be everywhere. He had to admit that he really didn't miss the bugs. Quickly entering the hospital through a maintenance door on the roof, he made his way toward Ronnie's floor. He forced himself to slow down his pace, although his emotions were driving him onward with excitement. Roy didn't want to draw any attention to himself by acting suspicious. He had come too far to get arrested by some over-zealous security guard.

After some friendly banter with the floor nurses and happily realizing that they thought he was his eldest son Brad, Roy walked down the hallway and into Ronnie's room. He knew that it would be hard to convince Ronnie where he had been and why he had left them all, but he had to try. She was the love of his life. If he couldn't convince her of that in the next few nights, the Mothership would have to leave him behind. Regardless of the consequences, Roy was prepared to stay on Earth the rest of his life and keep trying. He could not, would not fail. Both of their lives depended on it.

The room was dimly lit, but Roy could still see and hear her medical apparatus gently whirring and occasionally beeping. The odor of cleaning fluid was almost overpowering, as was the fragrance of the many potted plants and floral displays adorning the room. Ronnie was pretty much sedated, as she lay there in her pillow like hospital bed, looking to Roy as though she was dead. The updated photos onboard the ship had prepared him somewhat for that moment. Her long beautiful blond tresses had turned to white, and there was a care worn look on her face. He could hardly contain himself as grief over the lost years and her failing health washed over him. As he stood there softly sobbing, the urge to just grab her up in his arms was almost overpowering. Even though she was much older and the heart disease had ravaged her body, she was still the most beautiful woman that Roy had ever known. Ronnie groaned softly and rolled onto her side. Sensing Roy's presence in the room, she began to wake up. At first, thinking that he was Brad, Ronnie groggily spoke.

"Don't be sad, baby. Mama's going to be alright. Come give your old mom a hug."

Roy leaned over and gently gave her a hug. Wiping the tears from his eyes, he stood at the side of the bed holding her hand.

"What brings you back tonight? I thought you had flight training."

Roy stood there silently as Ronnie drifted back off to sleep. He would be unable to bring himself to disturb his sleeping angel this night. Roy didn't want to leave her again, but he knew he had to. Ronnie drifted back off to sleep and soon fell back into dream phase.

It was almost dawn when Roy made his way back to the survival module on the roof. Crunching his way back across the roof, he approached the module that was still in cloak mode. The scanners on board recognized his biological life force matrix and opened without making a sound. Sliding into the module's life sustaining jell, Roy's heart and bodily functions slowed to nearly zero.

During the long, hot California day, as Roy lay in stasis safely tucked away from all harm, a female security guard named Wanda and her trusty German shepherd, Bucky, slowly made the rounds of the hospital, including the roof. As the guard team approached the door to the hospital roof, the sensors on board the survival module sprang into action. The basic design parameters of this model of module were to cloak and evade any threats. If need be, it could even shoot into space in the event of a catastrophe of any sort, including total planetary destruction.

As the three year old German Shepherd Bucky and the middle aged female security guard Wanda crunched their way around the parameter of the hospital hoof, Roy was unaware of the apparent impending discovery of the module silently resting in the corner of the roof. Although the module was in cloak mode, completely invisible, the guard could stumble over it if it remained in place. The guard duo rounded the corner coming within feet of the cloaked module. The module then quickly and silently elevated to several feet above the guard team. Bucky stopped dead in his tracks and stood there staring at the seemingly empty cloudless sky.

"Come on, Bucky. We won't make our rounds on time if we don't get moving."

Hovering there for several seconds until they had passed, the module then softly returned to its former station.

***

Memories

As reality was silently slipping away, she found herself in a world between worlds. As Ronnie looked around the mist covered vistas of her dreamland, feathery pallid clouds drifted endlessly by in an azure sky and a slight cool breeze swept up the side of the mountain. Wild geese were winging their way northward to the ancestral nesting grounds to recuperate after a long hard migration, calling out to and being called by their fellow travelers with joyful honks. Several children were running to and fro on the emerald slope, chasing and being chased; their squeals of total abandonment and joy were music to a mother's ear. Farther across the mountain meadow, small family groups lay on colorful blankets, contently flying kites of all sizes and descriptions lofted into the cobalt sky on the gentle gusts of wind. The pleasant aroma of hamburgers and hot dogs cooking on beds of mesquite and hickory charcoal wafted across her senses like incense from the altar of God.

People were all around, familiar people, but Ronnie couldn't quite make out their faces. She knew this place but couldn't quite pinpoint the location. The mountainscape was beautiful beyond belief, and Ronnie was so entranced by its grandeur that any awareness of the approaching darkness had eluded her. The sun was setting quickly, causing the sky to turn a brilliant yellow orange hue that nearly took her breath away with its unbridled majesty. Ronnie would soon have to find her way back home, but how could she; there was no one to show her which way to go. Her hero, protector, and the love of her life had abandoned her. At times over the years, the sense of loss and grief for what could have been nearly drove her mad, but lately, for some odd reason, she had gained a modicum of peace. As the darkness once again closed in, Ronnie couldn't tell if she was waking up or going to sleep.

Then, there he stood, with the light from the hallway to his back. Ronnie couldn't make out his face, but his form was instantly identifiable. Questions made their way to the surface. Why was he here now? Why was he out of uniform? Why was he weeping? Drawing logic into view, she had come to the conclusion that the apparition standing in the twilight of her hospital room was her son and not the one person on the Earth that she longed the most to see.

The long buried memories began slowly circling in her subconscious. Like a spring storm building on the horizon, they came - some painful, some wonderful. She saw foggy glimpses of her wedding day, the vows that she shared with the man that had promised never to leave her, the birth of her children, and of the short life they had shared together in Indiana. Eventually, her thoughts gathered into a dark painful cloud. In the abyss of despair, Ronnie could see the day that she drove out of the driveway, never to see him again. Why did she do that? If she knew it would be the last time, she would have turned around. Why didn't she turn around? Was it anger or was it pride? Looking back, Ronnie regretted her decision. She could never have believed that at that point in time, they wouldn't be able to work things out. He was the love of her life. He still was. There never was anyone else. If only there would be another chance to make things work.

As her mind phased in and out of different parts of her life dredging up memories, her heart monitors began recording the tell tale signs of cardiac stress. Trying to pull the puzzle pieces of her life together, her mind moved on to the day that she had driven home in a pouring rain storm after talking to the F.B.I. agents all day about Roy's disappearance. What would she do? She was living with her mother. She had no income. The bills were piling up, and the mortgage was overdue. Ronnie remembered the hopeless feelings of that day. It was almost overwhelming. She had no friends, no money, and soon, no home to go back to. Ronnie remembered heading toward her mother's house, where she had been staying, but wished that Roy would come back in his right mind, take her and the kids home, sweep her up in his arms, and make the whole nightmare go away. With the children in the back seat, she drove around aimlessly for the rest of the day, partly to try and get her thoughts and plans together and partly avoiding going back to her mother's house.

Her relationship with her mother was tentative at best. Since the passing of Ronnie's father, her mother had become depressed and bitter. It seemed as though they argued about everything, from how to do dishes to when the kids should go to bed. What else could she do? Roy was gone, maybe forever, and there just wasn't much hope. And to be honest, she was afraid to go back to her house; Roy had acted so insanely strange before he disappeared. If he had come back, no telling what he might do.

***

Wakie!! Wakie!!

The sun sank over the Pacific seaboard, and the rain that had been pouring most of the afternoon subsided, leaving the air freshly scrubbed and a sunset that defied description with its brilliant hues of red, orange, and yellow cascading over the oceanscape in the far distance to the west. The time in the survival module had passed as though Roy had just blinked.

He was awakened by the familiar ringing of the old alarm clock, an action that he found to be quite amusing, since he wasn't really asleep. Roy laughed out loud. If only the rest of the world knew how truly humorous and kind his little Friends were, there wouldn't be any need for the secrecy and stealth that they had to employ. The popular view of extraterrestrials in most of Earth's media and literature is one of paranoia and mistrust, but, if these gentle souls had a hidden agenda, Roy couldn't find it. He couldn't help but hope that someday they would be able to welcome his world into their circle of self-control with the myriad of other progressing worlds they have already mentored. Until then, the subterfuge and diplomatic dance would continue.

Plausible deniability was something that would have to be overcome if Earth were ever to mature.

The danger was always in giving too much of a good thing too fast. If it wasn't done right, the world as we know it could fall into chaos and destroy itself. With great power, there must be great self-control. Roy knew it might take hundreds of years to achieve the level of self-control required for this to become a reality, but, for now, he could only hope. That was why they wanted him. He was the only one there at Devil's Tower that didn't have an agenda of some sort or other. They wanted to see if a completely unassuming soul like Roy could acquire the self-control that would be needed. He would be a diplomatic test case, of sorts, representing human kind. Of the 20 other humans on board this particular Mothership, only two were from the group taken aboard at Devil's Tower - one of them being an astronaut trained for the expedition, the other one being Roy. The remainder of the group was borrowed from various places and times, but all were still there of their own free will. The borrowed ones that had wished to return home were returned to their original state and age, having all recollection of the encounter removed from their memories, of their own volition, before being repatriated during the last Visitation. The other ten astronauts that boarded the ship at Devil's Tower were divided into teams and placed either on other cruisers or on Homeplanet. At the time, it was speculated that the popular Einstein theories of the correlation of time and the speed of light were correct and that there was little or no time gap, causing the borrowed ones not to age. Under normal conditions, this hypothesis would be correct. These were not normal circumstances, because, at the time, Earth's scientists were unaware of the Visitor's ability to compensate for the lap over of time and space. It was an innocent deception to keep the

Earth's "powers that be" from freaking out any more than they already had.

Chapter 4
Anger

Whispers

"B r a d... ohhh... B r a d... Wake up sleepy head. It's time to go fishing. Come on, buddy, it's a long way to the lake and we don't want to keep the catfish waiting."

Seven year old Brad jumped from his upper level bunk into the waiting arms of his doting father, knocking him to the floor.

"Wow, somebody's excited this morning!"

The two wrestled around for a couple of minutes, laughing and squealing with joy.

"Are Toby and Sylvia going with us?"

"Nope, they went with Mom to Grammas'. It's just you and me for the whole weekend. What do ya think about that, little dude?"

A deep peace filled Brads' subconscious. The love of his father washed over his soul, a feeling he hadn't experienced for many years.

"I love you, daddy!"

"I love you too, little buddy."

Brad woke from his impromptu nap around midnight thinking, "What the heck was that?"

The more he thought about it, the angrier he got. "Why would I have a stupid dream like that? Must be because of Mom."

He tried to shake it off but the melancholy and anger lingered for hours. Finally, exhaustion overwhelmed his anxiety and he drifted back off to sleep.

***

Then everything changed.

Ronnie had been driving around for hours, thought gathering and stress avoiding, when an announcer on the car radio called out her name.

"What was that? What was that?"

"I think he said that you won a house, Mama!"

"What!! What kind of house? Where? Did you hear, Brad?"

"No, Mama. Maybe they will say it again!"

It was a full hour before the story was repeated. Ronnie still remembered it, like it was yesterday.

"This is KJAR News, Southwest Indiana: The top story of the hour! A local woman, Jonnette Puckett, (Jonnette was her given name, but everyone called her Ronnie and Puckett was her maiden name) has won a dream house in a million to one chance raffle from the State of California. The announcement was given to us just about an hour ago. Apparently, the raffle officials have been trying to contact the lucky woman all day with no luck. If you know this woman, please have her call the station immediately!"

Ronnie listened intently as the announcer read her name and address again. It had to be her; she had never heard of anyone else that was named Jonnette, let alone Jonnette Puckett. The questions in her mind were: why weren't they using her married name, she hadn't been a Puckett for over ten years, and why were they using her mother's address? Oh well! She went to the station and claimed the prize anyway. Ronnie was ecstatic and befuddled. She really had won a house in California in a raffle that she didn't remember entering. That was well and good, but how would she get there? Maybe she could sell it. They could use the money. She remembered walking back out to the car; the whole experience had her shaken. She couldn't believe her luck, just when things seemed so hopeless.

"Are we moving to California, Mama?"

"No, children, we don't have the money to go to California."

Ronnie remembered deciding to pick up some groceries on the way back to her mother's house, but her mind was still reeling from the events of the day.

A house!! A house? In California, of all places! What am I going to do with a house in California? Boy! It would be great to get out of this state, away from all of the looks, whispers, and the uncomfortable silences when we walk into school and the grocery store. She had to find a way to do it! Her kids deserved a better life than that!

The rain that had been pouring down all morning intensified as she struggled to get the children and the groceries back into the old beat up station wagon. She was nearly exhausted as she plopped down in the driver's seat. The young mother sat there for several minutes thinking, rain water running down her face and dripping from her long blond hair. She looked at her rear view mirror, then out of her windshield before she reached for the ignition switch. Something caught her eye that instantly upset her.

"Great!!! Some kook put a flyer or something on our windshield! Brad, would you mind pulling that thing off?"

"But, Mom, it's raining!"

"You won't melt. Besides you're already soaked."

"Okay, but you're going to owe me!"

"Don't get fresh with me or you will be riding to Grandma's house on the roof rack."

"Cool! Can I?"

"No, just get the stupid thing off the windshield!!!"

Brad reluctantly jumped out of the car into the downpour, slipped and fell down, getting more completely soaked than before. He picked himself up, embarrassed and angry at himself, grabbed the offending piece of trash, and hurriedly scrambled back into the car.

"Look, Mom, it's a lottery ticket. Can I scratch it off?"

"Yeah, sure, today seems to be our lucky day. We supposedly won a house that we can't live in, and we could use a couple of million bucks! With our luck, the jackpot will be in rupees, and we will have to go to India to collect it! Well, it's going to be a long trip around the world, so make sure everyone has their seat belt on."

Ronnie pulled the station wagon out of the space in front of the grocery store and started down the street toward her mother's house on the outskirts of town. The rain by that time had become a torrent, making it very hard to see where she was going.

"Mom, what does it mean when all of the numbers match? And how much is a five with, uh, one, two, three, four, five, six zeros after it?"

Ronnie turned and looked in disbelief at the soggy lottery ticket that Brad was holding in his hand. It had to be a fake; there was no way that thing could be real! Her attention was suddenly drawn back to the rain washed road by the blast of air horns.

Directly in front of their old station wagon, and only about fifty feet away, was a diesel truck hydroplaning directly toward them and closing fast. Ronnie didn't even have time to scream before she instinctively jerked the steering wheel to the right, sliding the tank of a vehicle nearly sideways and back into the right lane. Although they barely avoided a collision with the huge tractor trailer rig, the desperate overcorrection caused the old vehicle to spin off the right highway shoulder and into a large, newly planted field. After almost flipping over and creating a small tidal wave of mud and seed potatoes, the nearly unrecognizable station wagon came to rest on all four wheels with a bounce that scattered groceries and toys all around the passenger compartment.

After franticly checking to make sure that her little family was all right and safe, Ronnie remembered looking at the nearly destroyed station wagon and laughing.

"Now that, boys and girls, is why we wear our seatbelts!"

Under the family's normal circumstances, the loss of the family car would have been devastating, but to say that their circumstances had changed was an understatement!

After finding the rain soaked lottery ticket stuck to her windshield, there would be more than enough money for the move to California and more than enough to live on the rest of their lives. Although it had been an amazing day, remembering the fight she had with her mother when she got home was still a hard thing to deal with.

"You are just running away again, like you did with Roy. You need to stay put! Did you ever think that he might come back?"

There had been more to the altercation, but all that Ronnie remembered was the words that hurt the most, "You are running away again, like you did with Roy."

Ronnie remembered deciding then and there that the little family would leave all of the pain and controversy behind. She bought a new car, had their last name legally changed to Smith, bought some new clothes, and headed for a new life. It had been a good decision. The children had thrived in their new home in California. They were grown now, and Ronnie was very proud them all: Sylvia, Toby, and Brad. Brad! Was that Brad who was here? She thought it was Brad! Could it be Roy? No. YES!!!!!!!!!

***

Mental fog

Gus had been on the streets for over two months. His hair was now long and matted. His beard was bushy and dirty. What was left of his clothes was in tatters, giving him the appearance of some sort of great shaggy dirty beast. His body was covered with scratches and scabs from crawling around under bushes and through drainage culverts. Although he had lost a great deal of weight, his muscular physique still made him an imposing figure, especially in the dark. The aluminum foil hat that he wore to keep the government from looking into his mind topped off the look of a mad man.

It was amazing how a person could seemingly, completely disappear into the underbelly of a city, if they didn't want to be found. He had quickly found out where to find food and shelter. Gus was one of the "invisible ones" that endlessly searched the darkness for the necessities of life. His paranoia had driven him away from forming any relationships, but kindred spirits among the homeless population knew about such things and were happy to point him in the right direction. Food and shelter might not mean the same things as most people in this country consider food and shelter to be, but, if it's all you can get when the whole world is against you, you will take what you can get and be thankful for it.

He was only able to overcome his paranoia long enough to keep from starving. Slipping silently out of his underground hiding place, he found food on a nightly basis, lovingly wrapped in plastic and left on top of the trash in the dumpster behind the diner. The other street people in the area were afraid of the "wild man," as they called him, even though he hadn't given them any reason to feed their fears. Just the sight of the dirty, ragged, muscular, hairy, silent, hulk of a man was enough for them to give him a wide berth and first choice at the dumpster.

The only bright spot in Gus's existence was watching the "woman in white," as he called her, walking up and down the sidewalk that ran between the diner where she worked and the apartment building where she apparently lived. He was strangely attracted to her, but his mental state prevented him from getting too close; he just couldn't trust anyone. Gus would stay out of sight and watch over her as he had done for the last two months since he spotted her heading home early one morning.

Maggie didn't know that she was being shadowed by a would-be attacker as she walked home in the pre-dawn mist. Her mind was numb after a long night of serving food and busing tables. All she was thinking about was getting a few hours sleep and then continuing her search for her long lost husband. Even though all of her friends had given up on the search and urged her to "move on," she knew in her heart that he was out there somewhere. Maggie was willing to look for him for the rest of her life if necessary.

The mugger silently closed in on Maggie, but, as he was about to make his move, a muscular arm reached out from the hedge that ran along the edge of the sidewalk and grabbed him by the throat. The scuffle was quiet and quite short as Gus applied a sleeper hold on the attacker, rendering him unconscious. Maggie temporarily awoke from her early morning stupor when she heard an unusual sound behind her. Being slightly startled, she turned around to look in the direction of the anomaly. "How strange," she thought. There was nothing there. The addled attacker woke up hours later inside a trash dumpster, sore and bruised but otherwise uninjured. The whole experience caused him to rethink ever coming back to that part of the city.

***

Painful memories

The monitor at the nurse's desk beeped loudly, and the charge nurse sprang into action. Ronnie's heart rate was dangerously high. Ventricular tachycardia wasn't something that her heart could handle.

Idiopathic Cardiomyopathy - Ronnie never thought she would hear those words when it concerned her personally. Idiopathic means without a known cause. Cardiomyopathy is a weakening or death of the heart muscle. Her mother died miserably fifteen years earlier from the disease, and her doctor had assured Ronnie that she couldn't inherit it from her mother. "Well, it just goes to show you that doctors don't know everything!" Ronnie had tried to convince herself and her family that everything would be all right, because the medicine of the day was much better than when her mother died. She had found out the hard way that, as an old friend had told her, "Some things just can't be fixed."

One thing Ronnie was thankful for, Cardiomyopathy usually moves slowly, sometimes taking years before it is detected, which gives its victims time to settle things before the end. Her mother's condition deteriorated over several years before she ended up in University Hospital waiting for a heart transplant. Even though her mother had died, she was glad for the time they had together. After Roy's disappearance, there had been a huge difference of opinion, separating Ronnie and her mother. A couple of years after the Smiths had moved to California, a friend of Ronnie's mother tracked her down and informed her of her mother's condition. Ronnie immediately hopped on an airplane and flew to her mother's side; there was no longer all the time in the world. Within a month, they had moved in together in Ronnie's new home on the west coast, all forgiven. It had been a good, but short, ten years.

Ronnie had been on the transplant list for six months. All she could do was wait for some poor soul to die and donate their heart. She had very mixed feelings about the whole thing, but there were more people to consider than just herself. Five years earlier, her world turned upside down after going for a routine stress test. The cardiologist in charge called her back into his office for a consultation the very next morning.

"We need to schedule an echocardiogram and an angiogram!"

"When do you want to schedule that?"

"Now, they are waiting on you in the Cath. Lab.

The rest of the day was a blur. Floating in a drug-induced euphoria, Ronnie remembered being placed on a cold operating table in a cold sterile room with several white clad personnel gathered around her. The pain of the procedure was intense but, thankfully, short lived. It was common practice to keep the patient in a semiconscious state for a shorter recovery time. The short meeting with the surgeon in the recovery room was devastating.

"It's Cardiomyopathy. I'm sorry. There was nothing we could fix."

Ronnie knew exactly what that meant; she had watched her mother die by inches.

Over the following months, Ronnie's condition was monitored closely by an unusually large team of cardiologists. After six months of treatment with pharmaceuticals, the conclusion was drawn that there wasn't any improvement. With no improvement, a pacemaker/defibrillator was implanted to stabilize her condition. There was an improvement of function, and her condition stayed relatively stable for three more years. Then for some unknown reason, which isn't unheard of, she started a downward spiral, falling into congestive heart failure several times before being put on the heart transplant list.

Love never gives up

The survival module gently rolled up to a vertical position allowing Roy to step out on to the hot roof. Upon touching a sensor on the outside of the module, it became invisible. With the touch of another sensor, his clothes once again changed. Although he didn't need any food or water while being protected by the module, it had been a long night, and he had been so preoccupied with seeing Ronnie that he had forgotten to eat anything. He would only need to eat a couple times per week because he was out of stasis only a few hours each day. As he stood on the roof admiring the sunset, a wonderful aroma wafted up to his position, drawing his attention to a railcar diner across the street close to the air base's main entrance.

The diner was a classic, just like the ones you would see in the movies. The owners had outdone themselves, adding dining room space on each end and behind the main car body turning the old railcar into a full-blown restaurant. The strategic placement of signage and shrubs disguised the fact that it was much larger than it appeared. Roy was concerned that he could be recognized as Brad, so his uniform of the day would be sandals, cutoff khaki pants, a tropical flower print island shirt, and, to complete the look, shoulder length blond hair crowned with a black bandana. Roy laughed out loud. His little Friends appeared to have picked up a Gilligan's Island episode or a Cheech and Chong movie for his disguise. He would make sure to get something tamer when he went to see Ronnie.

He crossed the street at the light to avoid any chance of an accident. The last thing he needed was to be ran down. Roy was confident that any damage he might experience could be repaired, but dead would be dead and no amount of medical technology could repair dead. Safely across the busy street, Roy entered the diner and looked around. The interior of the diner was decorated with hundreds of photographs and posters dating from World War I to present day. Hanging from the ceiling were fans made from actual airplane propellers. In the side dining areas, the floors were painted with the glossy gray commonly used on hanger floors, and the tables were made of recycled airplane wings. Completing the motif were chairs and benches made from military aircraft jump seats.

It was too late for the dinner crowd, and the diner was almost deserted except for a couple of low ranking military grunts. The aroma of cooking food made his mouth water. With all of the technology on board the ship, they still couldn't match the culinary nuances of the great American hamburger. A lot of things can be replicated from retrieved memory, but there was nothing like the real thing.

Roy hopped up onto one of the blue and chrome bar stools at one end of the long red counter. The diner was well maintained and impeccably clean. He could tell that the owner and staff had a great deal of pride in their establishment and their service. At the other end of the dining car, a beautiful young waitress was softly singing along with a song on the jukebox while gracefully mopping the floor. The fry cook had begun the mid-evening partial shutdown of the diner's immaculate kitchen. The steam from the carbonated water used to clean the grill billowed out into the dining area. Roy could almost sense his cholesterol level going up just sitting there. He was in fast food heaven.

"What can I get you, sweetie?"

The lilt of her voice was almost as intriguing as her perfume. Standing before him was the embodiment of the "American working woman." She was dressed in a fifties style white waitress uniform, complete with black work shoes, hose with a seam perfectly straight down the back of her legs. To top off the ensemble, she had an outrageous red and white polka dot bow fastened securely to the tightly wound bun hairdo on the back of her head. Looking at her standing there, Roy could see that she was tired, but it didn't dim her gentle infectious smile. Her nametag boldly proclaimed, "My name is Nancy, the friendliest waitress on the east coast." The tag was right! He would have to remember to give her a big tip.

As Roy sat there waiting for his order to come up, he couldn't help noticing the many unique photos hanging on the walls. One in particular caught his eye. There, directly in front of him, hanging over the doorway to the kitchen, was a brass framed portrait of Colonel Bradford R. Smith. He knew why the family had changed their name, but it was still disconcerting to see it there on the wall.

"He's a quiet one that one is! You always see stories about fighter pilots. They are always wild and crazy, but not that one. He is a real enigma."

"What do you mean an enigma?"

"Well! He flies a 50,000,000 dollar (it was actually 30,000,000 give or take a million) airplane that could blow up half a city, but he is totally devoted to his family, especially his mother. You can tell that he is always aware of what is going on around him, but he is so quiet that he sometimes seems to be a billion miles away. But that's all right. I like the strong silent type!"

"Sounds to me like you really like this guy."

"Oh yeah! All of the girls here do! If I thought I had half a chance with him, I wouldn't hesitate."

"Why don't you tell him how you feel?"

"I've dropped some hints, but he is so tied up with his family and career right now. Besides, he's in love with that one there, pointing to the opposite wall. He says that she is all of a girlfriend that he can handle right now. I think he just uses her as a defense mechanism."

Roy rotated on his bar stool, and there on the wall was a black and white picture of a young female flyer in her dress uniform, standing in front of a World War II P51 Mustang. He couldn't put his finger on it, but there was something familiar about her. Roy thought to himself, "I've got to find that boy a girlfriend!"

"Well, that's too bad for you I'm sure."

"Sure is, sweetie! You know something? You look a lot like him. Are you family?"

"Nope, never met the guy, but if I do I will send him to see you."

"Oh, he comes in a couple of times a week, but I guess I'm just not his type."

"Well, it is better to have loved and lost than to never to have loved at all."

"I don't know about that. See Margaret down there mopping her heart out (pointing to a coworker scrubbing the kitchen floor with a worn rag mop). She is desperately in love with her husband, Gus. Well, a while back, he just up and disappeared. No explanation, no goodbye, just gone! Makes you wonder if love is worth it at all."

"Well, you never know what happens in people's lives; there could be a good explanation."

"Yeah, you never know. I guess love conquers all."

"I truly hope so!"

Using some of the money that was in his wallet when he boarded the Mothership all those years ago, he was amazed at how much the price of a hamburger, onion rings and strawberry malt had increased over the years. Oh well, there was nowhere to spend money where he was going any way.

After eating what Roy considered to be food fit for a king, he thanked his waitress with a very generous tip and started to make his way back across the street towards the hospital. Standing at the edge of the street waiting for the light to change and watching the traffic pass, he was amazed at the diversity of the vehicles roaring up and down the street. Cars had really changed since he was last on Earth. Roy chuckled as he thought about how crude and uninteresting they were compared to the simplest shuttlecraft on board the Mothership.

The light seemed as though it would never change, and his thoughts wandered back to the diner and the emotional pain that Margaret was experiencing at the disappearance of her husband, Gus. A wave of sorrow and regret once again washed over his soul. Even though he wasn't totally at fault for the events that Ronnie had to deal with, he knew that the pain she and his children had endured was his responsibility. Roy had gone over it in his mind thousands of times over the years and had come to the conclusion that, even though the implanted vision had possessed his mind, he could have said no. If he had known that he would be gone this long, he would have said no!

***

Sweet confusion

The nurse's station on the cardiac floor was buzzing with activity as usual, in anticipation of a shift change. The day and night shift charge nurses were quietly discussing doctor's orders, patient reports, and the work assignments for the rest of the floor nursing staff.

It had been another long hard day, but it was more than the work or the paycheck that inspired their dedication to the healing profession. It was mostly the knowledge that they were making a difference in the lives of their patients and the hope that, if they were in the same position, someone would do their best for them. The care for patients also included familiarizing themselves with their families and friends. This was one aspect of nursing that both of the charge nurses enjoyed the most.

"Mrs. Smith sure has a good son. Ever since she has taken a turn for the worse, he has been here every morning and every evening!"

"Sometimes twice a night too; I saw him in here at 2:00 A.M. this morning! Isn't he a flyer or something like that?"

"Yeah! He's a fighter pilot, a Colonel in the Air Force."

"He must be on leave or something. He hasn't been here this much before."

"I don't think he's on leave. My nephew is in flight school under him, and he tells me that Colonel Smith is training them on night operations."

"That's strange. How can he be in two places at one time?"

"Okay, how about this, my Colonel Bradford is about 5' 10", even though he looks to be over 6 foot in that uniform of his. He has blue eyes that look right through you and that curly black hair. Mmmm."

"That sounds like him."

"Doesn't she have three kids? Maybe one of her other sons is visiting on my shift."

"Colonel Smith told me that his brother and sister are in really remote locations on opposite sides of the globe. I think he said that one was in Alaska, and the other is on some volcanic island in the southern hemisphere. He told me that they would be here if they could."

"Well! They had better get here soon!"

"He has been trying to contact them for the last few days, but so far no luck!"

"He seems to be holding up good though. It must be his military training!"

"He's married, I can tell. He hasn't said so, but I can read the signs."

"He doesn't act married around the girls on days! He doesn't say much, but the way he doesn't say much, wow!"

"I don't know; he might be using humor as a release mechanism. He sure is a funny guy. He always has something hilarious to say."

"Are we talking about the same guy? Colonel Smith is the most reserved and serious man I have ever met, and he always looks so good in that uniform of his too."

"That's funny. I have never seen him in a uniform. He is always in regular street clothes, and, to be honest, he could use someone to give some fashion direction, if you know what I mean! "

"Don't you girls have some work to do?"

"Yes, Head Nurse Lake!"

"Yes, Head Nurse Lake!"

Head Nurse Lake started to walk away, hesitated, then turned and smiled.

"One more thing, Ladies!"

"Yes, Head Nurse Lake?"

"If I was 20 years younger, I would give that man a run for his money! Maybe even show him how to dress!"

The nurses stood silently in amazement as Head Nurse Lake walked away.

"Wow! That was unexpected! Well, like she said, we have work to do."

The night charge nurse pulled up Ronnie's chart, and a surprised look came across her face."

"Will you look at that! Mrs. Smith is being transferred to the base hospital tonight, but there isn't a specific time listed. How weird!"

***

Gus had a miserable day; the rain that had fallen in the afternoon had flooded the storm drain system forcing him and all of the other street people out of their temporary "homes" and into the "real world". He spent the day huddled under an overpass monitoring the water levels. When it was safe to go "home," he resumed his "normal" activities of scurrying through the drainage tunnels that honeycombed the city streets, searching dumpsters for food, hiding from all of those that he deeply believed were pursuing him, and watching for "the woman in white." He was rewarded for his diligence as the sun went down and the streetlights blinked on.

Gus was glad that he could come out of his storm drain hiding place. He crawled out of the drainage pipe that he used to cross under the street running between the hospital and the diner that Maggie worked in. Popping up behind the hedges that ran around the parameter of the hospital, Gus took up a position with the best vantage point to keep an eye on this angel that he had found. He wasn't sure why he was obsessed with this woman. Something about her was vaguely familiar. Gus watched her make her way down the block and into the diner.

The voices in his head were raging, screaming out all manner of nonsense. Sometimes there were so many voices that he couldn't understand any of them. Gus sat in the dark watching Maggie go about her nightly tasks. As he sat there in the dark, another man joined him behind the hedge. The man was dressed in some sort of pirate costume which included an eye patch and wooden leg. The apparition for some reason sounded exactly like Gus's long dead grandfather.

"Why don't you go to her?"

"She wouldn't like me."

"You're probably right; you are nothing! You are less than nothing"

Then what appeared to Gus to be an orangutan dropped in behind the hedge on the other side of him and began to speak.

"If you go to her, the police will beat you. Do you want her to see you get a beating like some filthy animal?"

"Shut up! Just shut up!"

Gus was alone again, as he had been the entire time. By then he had become accustomed to the voices and the hallucinations; they had become his constant companion. As his condition had worsened, it had become harder and harder to tell who was real and who was not. Gus was wondering that very thing when a man started to run across the road at the light. The man was dressed oddly, and he was sure that he was a hallucination. The voices in his head were raging again, and he was content to just sit and watch until suddenly one voice out shouted all the others. It came across with such force and clarity that all of the others faded away.

"Follow him!"

***

The light turned to walk, and, as Roy started to step off of the curb, a voice deep in his mind shouted at him.

"NO!"

He froze in place as a large truck ran the light, passing just inches from where he was standing. Roy was still shaking as he ran across the street. He was very glad that he was being monitored by his Friends on Mothership. Getting killed at this point would be a great disappointment, after all that they had done to make this whole thing happen.

It was after visiting hours so Roy had to go in through the emergency entrance at the rear of the hospital. Walking around the corner of the building, he discovered that the streetlights were out and the walkway was dark. Gus scrambled to his feet and silently stepped out of the hedge. As Roy pushed on toward the back of the building, he heard footsteps quickly closing in on his position. Gus quickly and quietly closed in on the hallucination or man in front of him. He honestly didn't know at that point weather he would speak to the man, attack the man, or run away from the man.

Roy turned around just in time to catch a glimpse of a fine thread-like blue beam of light extending from his survival pod, silently floating in its position on the corner of the roof, to the back of his pursuer's head. The huge man was now standing dead still in the darkness. Gus had suddenly stopped in his tracks.

"What just happened?"

Gus was suddenly thinking with a clarity of mind that he didn't remember ever having. He was shaking with excitement as he pulled the aluminum hat from his head that he wore to keep the C.I.A. from reading his thoughts and dropped the ground. Where was he? Why was he here? Who was that man ahead on the sidewalk? Why was he smiling at him? These were questions that Gus desperately needed to have answered, but not now. There was something else that he needed to do. But what was it? As the beam twinkled out, Gus, the would-be attacker, turned and wandered off down the sidewalk. He raised his gaze from the ground to the diner across the street.

"No! It couldn't be! Yes! Yes!! Yes!!! Maggie!!! Maggie!!!! Maggie!!!!!"

Roy stood there in amazement as the man suddenly ran across the street and into the diner, narrowly avoiding being run down by a trash truck. Despite the noise of the traffic and the garbage truck operator yelling at the top of his lungs, Roy could still hear the man calling out, "Maggie!!! Maggie!!! Maggie!!!" as he burst through the diner's front door. Suddenly one of the waitresses ran across the dining room and leaped into his waiting arms.

After going on to the emergency entrance and up to the hospital roof for a quick wardrobe change, Roy moved on to meet his greatest challenge. He was hoping to fare at least as well as the crazy man that had just run across the street.

***

What doesn't kill you....

After many months of rehabilitation, Billy and his mother, Melissa, were released from the hospital with no place to go. The small fortune (made in the Oklahoma oil fields) that his father had left them was completely depleted by their hospital and rehab bills. Not knowing what to do or where to go, the young mother reluctantly agreed to marry her physical therapist, Ben Kenny, who had been by her side since her arrival at the small hospital.

Wayne Kenny's father, Ben, appeared to be a good man and seemed to be exactly what Melissa and baby Billy needed so, after an extended time of recovery, she married him. Three years after their marriage, Wayne was born. He was beautiful and strong nearly perfect as human children go despite being born with only one hand.

Ben, being a bit of a dreamer, soon moved his wife Melissa, baby Billy, and infant Wayne to Alaska in search of something, but he never appeared to be sure what that actually was. It could have been the down turn in the economy, his inability to capture his dream, or some deep seated mental disease that caused him to begin drinking heavily, abuse prescription drugs, and exhibit violent outbursts. Try as she must, Melissa (still suffering from injuries sustained in the plane crash) was unable to stabilize the household situation and their lives became increasingly miserable. Nearing destitution because of his "disease," nearly everything that the little struggling family had went to Ben's addiction, even going as far as pawning the boys' Christmas toys given to them by relatives in Texas and a local Church group.

When times got bad, Billy and Wayne just simply stayed out of sight. They soon learned how to survive for days at a time in the wilderness, catching and collecting whatever they could. By the ages of 6 and 8, Billy and his brother were very adept at living off the land.

The fact that Wayne had been born without a left hand due to amniotic band syndrome didn't hamper him at all. If there was something that Wayne didn't think that he would be able to do, Billy would put his own arm behind his back and prove that it could be done. Billy was the best half brother that Wayne could have possibly had. To make life almost unbearable, their mother, the one bright spot in the boy's lives, passed away when they were 10 and 12 years old. Within a year of her death, what was left of the man that their mother had married was in prison. Going to jail actually was a fortunate break for him. If not for being arrested when he was, he would have been dead too! At eleven and thirteen, all the boys had left to rely on was each other. Their ordeal formed an unbreakable bond between the half brothers that knew no limits. Soon after their mom passed, a retired Army general noticed them wandering in the town and tracked them to an abandoned cabin in the forest. Then, when Wayne's father went to jail, he took them out of the wilderness and off of the streets; the old soldier gave them the best home they had ever known and best chance for survival that they had ever had.

Over the course of several years, Wayne's father completed his time in the "Alaska State Extended Stay" (prison), getting out early for good behavior. By that time he had become a born again Christian and had been sober for six years. After settling into his new life, he tried to reconnect with Billy and Wayne, but their lives were heading in directions that he couldn't follow. Ben Kenny was heartbroken when he realized that, although God had forgiven him for the depraved life that he had lived, the people that he had hurt the most wouldn't be able to. He lived an exemplary life, until his death two years later from residual damage done by past drug abuse, helping fellow addicts find a better life. He continued to the end trying to make amends with his sons.

After high school, Bill joined the Marines and moved up the ranks quickly. When he made Sergeant, he felt at home with his grade and decided to re-up for four more years. After two tours of duty in Indochina, Bill thought about mustering out until Wayne gave him a call to tell him about a special operations unit that was being formed for world security.

Barry's step father, Sergeant Bill "Nuke'm High" Taylor, nicknamed by his half brother Wayne Kenny for his attitude concerning the extraterrestrials, was a real piece of work by some people's standards. He was a Marine's Marine, gung ho to the max. Don't take it wrong, there is a place and a time for that kind of man, and it had been exactly the right time and place for him to be in Barry and his mother's lives.

Being one of the hundreds of security personnel with top secret clearance at Devil's Tower during the last Visitation, he had originally been assigned as a protector for Barry and his mother. Chosen for his loyalty, combat skills, and ability to think on his feet, the muscular 6' 3" Marine Drill Sergeant was the perfect man for the job. Even though he was very rough on the outside, he possessed a nobility of spirit and dedication to honor that was irresistible to Barry's mother, Jillian. She would always say, "I never had a man look at me with such kindness and compassion, those piercing blue eyes looked right into my soul." Jillian had been mistreated most of her adulthood and, until Bill came into her life, had never known real honest love.

Sergeant Bill soon found that the "assignment" would take a turn that he never expected. For all of their differences, he soon fell in love with her also. To the surprise of even his half brother Wayne and superiors, they married three months after their first meeting.

"Now that is going over and above the call of duty, Brother!"

Wayne, being unable to join the armed forces due to his physical handicap, had put his energies into academics, majoring in criminal forensics. With an I.Q. rating over 140, he graduated university studies in two years with honors. The World Defense Corps or W.D.C. (a civilian, military cooperation) recruited him after finishing graduate school. After years of intensive grooming and training, he achieved top secret status and was eventually put in charge of operations at Area 51. With an emphasis on interstellar communications and diplomacy, Wayne was a perfect fit with the W.D.C. Although he never would admit it, Sergeant Bill and Wayne always suspected that the old General had pulled some strings.

Two of only three outsiders on "the site" that witnessed the "event," the rest being government or military personnel sworn to silence, Barry and Jillian (known to the super secret government operatives in charge of securing the situation as "the package") had to be isolated, silenced, and protected. The government assets and military leadership were nearly overwhelmed with the arrival of the extraterrestrials, but the possibility that there would be civilian witnesses was more than they could have planned for; let alone a young woman and small child.

Wayne and Sergeant Bill, drawing on their training and experience, quickly took control of the task at hand. He couldn't have imagined it at the time, but, for Sergeant Bill, the task at hand would not only prove to be the most difficult and rewarding assignment of his life but, in retrospect, it would become the joy of his existence.

Barry was a precocious child and his mother, Jillian, being alone in the world except for her only child, greatly appreciated their new found fortune. They would never again worry about where their next meal was coming from or how they were going to keep a roof over their heads.

The world's governments were willing to go to any lengths and any expense to conceal the secret that they felt could throw the world's populations, especially the "religious" populations, into total chaos. It was their consensus that to have proof positive that we are not alone in the universe would be devastating to the human psyche. Others believed that the government should trust the human spirit and mankind's ability to cope with the most extreme situations, but they were simply shouted down, censured, and sworn to silence under penalty of death.

Being the recipient of a Congressional medal of honor for bravery under fire, Sergeant Bill Taylor was no stranger to war. Even though this was a peace time assignment, he was always prepared for the worse. At their home in the back woods of Idaho far from the encroachments of almost any possible intruders, Sergeant, as Barry and his mom Jillian called him, had built a large array of security systems all funded by "anonymous" donors from around the world.

The main house was quite nice - a 3,000 square foot, six-bedroom, four bath, Bavarian lodge style, log, "A" frame, set back from the main road almost a mile. The whole complex was solar and hydrothermally powered and completely off the grid. From the weather vane on the roof to the foundation, their "little cabin in the woods" seemed to be a perfectly normal, although upper level, home.

Beneath the main structure, blasted out of solid base rock and centered around an elevator that serviced the three upper levels of the home, lay a reinforced bunker that could resist nearly any violent strike imaginable. The walls and ceiling were six feet thick, reinforced with steel and lined with Kevlar armor. Four escape corridors ran approximately a half mile from the main bunker complex to smaller bunkers placed on opposite corners of the property. In each of the small bunkers, there was an assortment of weapons ranging from hand guns to laser guided missiles. Access to the bunkers was via a high speed tram system similar to a roller coaster track that could take the occupants to safety at over 60 miles per hour.

In the event that it was better to flee rather than fight, in each of the bunkers there was an armored all terrain vehicle (A.A.T.V.) that looked like a scaled down Striker assault tank, fueled and ready to go at all times. During the evacuation phase, the other three A.A.T.V.s would also burst out of their respective escape tunnels, serving as decoys, guided remotely by the master computer located deep within the bunker control room.

Around and inside of the parameter fence of the 2,000 acre reserve were remotely controlled pop-up turrets containing pedestal mounted machine guns, smoke generators, and rocket propelled grenade launchers.

If there was to be a complete breakdown of all of the security measures, there was a failsafe system, a vehicle of last resort, actually five in total - one in the house and one each in the outer bunkers - built similar in function to an ejection seat in a fighter aircraft but on a larger more powerful scale, shaped like the nose cone of a rocket. In these short-ranged escape "pods," there was room for three to be rocketed approximately 25 miles to a predetermined place of rescue or escape. Again, like the A.A.T.V.s, all of the last resort rockets would fire simultaneously in opposite directions to serve as decoys. From there, a system of unmapped safe houses and secret bunkers were available, and Sergeant Bill knew them all.

Barry didn't know about the precautions and the reasons behind the precautions until after his mother died. Jillian, on the other hand never became aware of the fact that she and her only son Barry were the most endangered people on Earth. She rested well at night just knowing that Sergeant Bill was by her side. Unbeknownst to Barry and Jillian, there were people in this world that desperately wanted to use them for some advantage, real or imagined, calculating to force the world's governments, military organizations, intelligence communities, and, they presumed, the Visitors themselves, to do their bidding. In some people's minds, to have that kind of control would be the ultimate prize.

Sergeant Bill Nukem High Taylor not only felt that Barry and Jillian should be protected from evil Humans but from the Aliens also. He had a general distrust of almost everyone on the planet and off. Bill, from the beginning, had voiced his opinion about the Visitors. He felt that there was a hidden agenda behind their benevolent facade, and that we should Nukem high at the first hint of trouble. Since the death of his wife, the deep seated resentment for the off-worlders boiled to the surface. Even though there was no basis for his hatred, he blamed Them for Jillian's death. He had to blame someone.

Chapter 5
Reconciliation
Lights Out

Normally, every time the power fluctuated, the backup generator would instantly start up to insure a constant power flow. That is, if there was enough fuel to operate the generators and if the power lines from the generator shack didn't go down too. Combined with the main battery backup and the internal batteries for the computers and communications, Sylvia had complete confidence that she could work until she dropped.

It had been a long, hard six months, and the rest of the staff had flown home for a well-deserved rest. The work wasn't the only reason that Sylvia was putting in the long hours, although the work was what she lived for. Along with trying to map the entire face of Planet Earth, she was helping to monitor a dangerous situation in the tropics of the southern Indian Ocean. The satellite uplink that she used to accumulate data for mapping could also be used for surveillance. The resolution of the orbiting photo satellite was great enough to read a newspaper from space, and the G.P.S. system could measure changes in the Earth's crust to less than a millimeter. Her brother Toby was on a volcano watch station in an area that was becoming more volatile by the minute. Although he didn't think so, Toby needed all the help that he could get.

To complicate things, Sylvia had just received a disconcerting email from her older brother, Brad. The message about her mother was bad enough, but now she could see that the mountain was about to blow and the satellite phone wouldn't work. Sylvia needed to be by her mother's side; it might be her last chance to say goodbye, but, if she was going to be able to help Toby escape through the maze of jungle trails in time, she knew that she would have to stay on station. Then everything went black.

"Oh, man! You would think that NASA could find a facility that wouldn't go dark every time the wind blows!!"

Sitting there in the glow of the emergency lighting, Sylvia decided to wait out the storm before dragging out the old extension cable.

***

Love's Quest

"Colonel Smith! You here again?"

"I couldn't stay away from my favorite girls."

"You sure are a good son. I wish my kids cared as much as you do."

"I am sure that they do. You'll find out when you need them. How could they not love a sweetheart like you? Speaking of sweethearts, how is mine doing tonight?"

The ageing nurse blushed and small tears filled the corners of her twinkling eyes. No one was ever that nice to her, not even her husband of 38 years. She quickly regained her composure.

"According to her chart, she got pretty agitated early this morning for some reason, and she had to be sedated to keep her heart rate at a safe level. She is doing better than this morning when you saw her. She is sleeping naturally now since the sedation has worn off."

"Thanks for taking such good care of her."

"It's our pleasure, Colonel Smith."

Before he knew it, he was once again standing at Ronnie's bed side. This time, he was able to keep his composure as he watched his loved one sleep. Roy stood there for what seemed like an eternity pondering what he would say to her. He had run through it a thousand times in his mind, now he didn't know how to start.

Ronnie had begun to feel at ease with her dreams by the time the person that the nursing staff believed to be Brad had gotten to her bedside. Ronnie struggled to wake up, but then, as the drugs over took her conscious will, she rolled over on her side facing the window and slipped back into her dream world. Roy was relieved as Ronnie quieted and slipped peacefully into a sound sleep. He stood by her bedside for two more hours and was about to retire to his hiding place on the hospital roof when she stirred and then rolled over and looked up into Roy's tear reddened eyes.

"I didn't think that I was dreaming. I always knew you would come back."

Roy was beside himself with joy. It was the voice that Roy had yearned to hear for 30 years, the voice of an angel. This was more than he could have dreamed of. The questions on Roy's heart and mind were whether she would take him back and whether she would go with him. When Ronnie was strong enough, she would know everything, but, for now, he would have to take it slow.

"There is a lot that I have to tell you, my love, things that you probably won't believe, but, first, let me start by telling you that I never stopped loving you. I never stopped wanting you. The hardest thing that I have ever done was to be away from you and the children. Please believe me. It was not my choice to be gone so long."

Ronnie listened intently to Roy as he spoke slowly and meticulously. Over the next two hours, Roy laid out the story, beginning at his obsession with the implanted vision and the decision to blindly take that fateful flight into the cosmos, not knowing that he would be gone so long, to where he had been all these years and why he had to come back. Although he was terrified that Ronnie might say no, Roy steeled his nerves and asked the most important question of his life.

"The question is this, my love. Will you join me among the stars?"

In a voice, feeble but confident, the answer lovingly came. "Yes!"

***

Same song, second verse

After a good night's rest and another long day at the hospital watching his mother sleep, Brad returned to the air base and went through the customary preparations for night flight training with his four Smurflings in tow. He was thinking, "Well, let's try this again." But he didn't let his frustration show to his crew or the tower.

"AF037, Infield One, request start up."

"AF037, Infield One, clear for start up, Papa Smurf"

Checking that the throttles were all the way back to the idle position, he started the right hand engine and waited for the R-GEN light to extinguish on the warning panel, then started the left hand engine. As the L-GEN light twinkled out, he began checking the engine revolutions. Both engines were spooling up beautifully. The canopy closed and latched with a clunk to shut out the quickly increasing noise. Brad keyed up the encrypted secure voice activated communication system.

"If all lights are green, then wheels up, Smurflings!

Colonel Brad, thinking that he heard a laugh from one of his trainee pilots, barked an order over the radio.

"There are over a hundred Smurfs, which one do you want to be?"

None of the pilots answered.

"That's what I thought!"

Actually, Brad considered it an honor because over his career as a flight instructor he had trained hundreds of excellent pilots.

Brad then lowered the aircrafts flaps to the full down position, proceeded to turn on the anti-collision lights, and then made another check of all indicators and gauges. A little "wing flapping" of the control surfaces, a check of weapons guidance systems, and it was go time! With a light push on the throttles, the engines spooled up to seventy percent on the R.P.M. gauges. Before he even released the ground parking brake control, the Colonel always took the time to visually check the runway and airspace. Although this was a scheduled flight, safety was ultimately each individual pilot's responsibility.

After rechecking the controls, he called the tower again.

"Tower AF037, Infield One, request permission to taxi."

"AF037, Infield One, permission to taxi. Proceed to runway one five."

The jet began to move as Brad eased the throttles forward. He then throttled back the idle to drop the planes inertia and performed a required landing and taxi brake check. Advancing the throttle again, Brad smoothly made his way through the labyrinth of taxiways to the intersection with runway one five, being sure not to stop with the fighter's nose extending past the edge of the runway. After a catastrophic accident early on in military aviation, the "watch your nose" rule had been strictly enforced.

One more recheck of traffic, gauges, and controls.

"Tower AF037, Infield One, request take off."

"AF037, Infield One, cleared for takeoff runway one five."

The Colonel made a smooth right turn to the center of the runway, wasting no space, for space behind an aircraft was worthless. He thought to himself, this was going to be another perfect takeoff!

Brad applied the brakes, rechecked the gauges, flaps, and controls, and then did a little more "wing flapping." He was looking forward to being airborne again. The scream of the turbines, the feel of the controls, the rush of adrenalin that came every time he went wheels up, was worth all of the years of study and training that, at times, seemed endless.

Pushing the throttle forward to one hundred percent R.P.M., Brad released the brakes. The gravitational forces pushed him tightly into the form-fitted seat as he pushed the throttles to full afterburner. All thoughts of the problems on the surface of the Earth temporarily disappeared as the fighter roared down the runway. The marker lights along the sides of the tarmac nearly became a blur before they dropped out of sight, as Brad eased back on the stick and pointed the fighter sky ward. In mere seconds, he and the four trainees were in the air, forming up in a V formation behind him. After giving a loud war cry, Colonel Brad keyed his microphone and spoke in a much more professional voice.

"And, gentlemen, that is how it's done!!!!!!!"

The sound level was deafening without the use of proper hearing protection, but that was just one of the plethora of things that Colonel Bradford Smith loved about the life he was living. If it was loud and fast, he loved it.

Colonel Bradford Smith, why on Earth did his mother choose Smith, when there were so many other boring names to choose from? Why not Santini or Rickenbacker or, well, anything else but Smith?

As a young man, aviation was just about the only thing that Brad had been interested in, since the move to California that is. Their new home was at the edge of the largest Air Force base in the state, which only served to fire his desire all the more.

Brad had also gotten involved in the "World Explorers" organization for boys, and, because of his love for flying, he was paired with a highly decorated combat pilot, who unbeknownst to Brad had top secret clearance and ties to Area 51.

Brad excelled in his scholastic studies and by senior year he had become commander of the Flight Rangers, a R.O.T.C. type program that had been organized by his old friend and mentor from the X Boys, as they called themselves. After graduating high school, he was accepted into the Air Force academy in Colorado. Upon graduating from academy with honors, he was assigned to the fighter training wing based in California, the same wing that had been under the command of his old mentor. The duty assignment pleased Brad very much. Of late, his mother had fallen on bad health, and the proximity of the base to the hospital made it possible for him to remain in the elite fighter group, while still monitoring his mother's health and well-being.

Brad had accomplished much in his lifetime, more than most men his age could dream of. The things he had done and seen were almost beyond belief, but there was always something deep inside his soul, something missing - the acceptance of a father. That acceptance was not possible and he knew it, but he yearned for it nonetheless, as we all do. He would once again, as he often did, push it to the back of his mind before the sorrow and frustration turned to anger.

***

Into the wild blue

Colonel Bradford Smith ordered the fighter group to head west toward the coast and climb to 25,000 feet, then level off, being sure to stay subsonic over land. In less than 15 minutes, they were over the Pacific Ocean, where Colonel Brad ordered the group to climb to 70,000 feet and increase their speed to Mach 2.1 (approximately 1,540 miles per hour) to give the trainees a taste of the capabilities of the Warbirds. The Warbirds that the training group was flying had the capability of achieving more than Mach 3, sustainable for short durations, and then only under clearance orders.

The sun was nearly over the horizon, and the sky was ablaze with color. Even though there was a cloud bank moving in, the sunset was stunning. Beams of sunlight pierced the clouds like laser beams, with a brilliance that could blind the unprotected eye.

After receiving clearance from control to perform maneuvers over shipping lanes, Brad began his run. Three minutes and 25 miles beyond the coastline, he ordered the group to decrease their speed to Mach 1 and drop below radar range. Approximately 200 miles further west, Brad ordered the fighter group to slow to fighting speed (below the speed of sound which is approximately 767 miles per hour) and then turn north parallel to the coast that was completely out of visual.

"Gentlemen, just a reminder, some of the conditions of this test are computer generated, but the darkness and danger is real. Stick together. Your lives depend on team work. What you learn tonight will save your life in a combat situation. Stay on your toes and don't take any unnecessary chances. I can't emphasize enough; learn all you can during these simple exercises. There will be time later for Mach 2 vector rolls, which were aileron or barrel rolls performed in a curve or vector, and high YoYo's (starting with level wings, pulling up hard to gain altitude over the top inverted, looking down on the enemy then turning toward and behind, lining up for a kill shot). We will delve deeply into the career and tactics of, among others, Brigadier General Robin Olds, a triple ace serving in WWII and Vietnam, who, as you know, is the father of supersonic dog fighting. Your orders are, as we previously discussed, to remain at subsonic (below the speed of sound), fly 500 nautical miles north by 10 degrees west, then proceed due east for 50 miles, where you will climb to 30,000 feet. After achieving altitude, proceed 200 miles east. At that point, bear south by 10 degrees east. If you aren't lost by then, return to base! Need I repeat? Do not, I say again, do not exceed the speed of sound over any populated areas! Good luck, you are on your own gentlemen! Try not to embarrass me or yourselves! Colonel Bradford Smith, out".

Colonel Brad chuckled to himself knowing what the young trainees were up against. Over the next couple of hours, the trainees will encounter warning lights, false instrument readings, power outages, and near total darkness. They will have to fly with instruments, without instruments, by the stars, and dead reckoning. At times only one will have instruments, and the others will have to stay in tight formation, trusting their wing man with their lives.

Colonel Brad Smith pushed the throttle forward punching the air speed up to Mach 2, performed a perfect aileron roll (an aerial maneuver in which the aircraft rotates on its axis and continues on a straight line) and then pulled back on the controls. The Warbird responded obediently. Pointing the nose of the fighter toward the Moon, Brad could feel the pressure from his flight suit inflating as he kicked in the afterburners and engaged the "hyper-thrust drive" (a super secret thrust multiplier rumored to be of alien origin).The aircraft quickly broke through the cloud cover and into the star filled night sky. This was what he lived for; the pure joy of total freedom. As much as he loved being an Air Force officer and the opportunities it afforded him, he still dreamed of going into space some day.

From his vantage point in the cockpit, Brad could see the curvature of the Earth and the terminus at the edge of space, a maneuver only made possible by the latest version of top secret hyper-thrust drive (the real designation was classified) that had been installed in his upgraded aircraft. Only with the addition of the hyper-thrust drive could his aircraft surpass what was called "coffin corner" (a point at which the speed of an aircraft is overtaken by altitude and gravity causing it to stall and fall toward Earth), which would be for his aircraft approximately 76,000 feet. The mere sight of the blackness of space and the yearning to explore it always gave him pause.

Brad cut the afterburners, spooled back the hyper-thrust drive, leveled out, and slowed to subsonic. The stars were so much more brilliant from high altitude far from city lights. It was always bittersweet to have to start his decent, but he knew that no man-made aircraft could sustain flight without some kind of energy, and the fuel onboard his aircraft was limited. Brad had calculated that he could slow to a leisurely 150 miles an hour, point the aircraft's nose down 10 degrees, and practically coast the rest of the way to the Nevada border. He had planned on continuing due east across the Sierra Nevada mountain range, fully intending to make a wide radius south across Death Valley then back to base. The advantages of rank did have their privileges.

***

The clock is ticking

Deep within Roy's brain, Ronnie's answer triggered more than an emotional response; it also triggered a subconscious signal, a password if you will, opening a very minute, but substantial, telepathic pathway.

"Yes, Roy?"

"My friend, it's time to gather my chickens."

Within minutes of Ronnie's acceptance of Roy and his plan, the waiting extraction team was on the move. Seeming to appear out of nowhere, two men and two women dressed in military medical uniforms silently pushing a specially built gurney exited the hospital service elevator directly across from the nurse's station. A tall slender woman who was obviously in charge of the group stepped up to the nurse's duty desk.

"Head Nurse Lake, we are here to transfer a patient to the base hospital. Here are the appropriate documents for said transfer."

"Yes, Ma'am, we have been expecting you. I will have my nurses prepare her for transport."

"That won't be necessary. My team will take care of everything. Also, Colonel Smith has given us orders to allow the nursing staff to give their well wishes to his mother before she leaves. He said to tell you thank you for taking such good care of his mother. We must move quickly, time is of the essence."

Head Nurse Lake quietly paged the remaining nurses and orderlies that were on duty and advised them of the situation, telling them to meet her at the duty desk.

The extraction team quickly pushed on down the hallway and into Ronnie's hospital room leaving the two male medics standing outside while the two females entered closing the door behind them. Once inside, the lead female pulled a device that looked similar to a small electronic tablet from her uniform pocket and started touching icons. The other female busied herself disconnecting monitors, drip lines, oxygen hoses, and anything else that wasn't necessary for the move.

Roy was still holding Ronnie's hand as she drifted off to sleep.

"Hold on, my love. It will be better soon."

"Well, ladies, it's show time."

Roy moved away from Ronnie's bedside and stood with his back to the door. The lead female touched another icon on the small electronic device in her hand, while the second female attendant turned the covers down on the unusual gurney. Slowly and ever so gently, Ronnie began to levitate from her hospital bed, floated over and above the gurney, and then softly came to rest in her new bed. As soon as Ronnie was tucked in, Roy opened the door, and the whole entourage silently and gently began making its way down the hallway toward the service elevator.

A small group of well-wishers had gathered at the duty desk to say good bye, most of them thinking that the beautiful, kind, genteel lady they had cared for over the last few months probably wouldn't be alive much longer. The group was so focused on their patient and friend, that no one noticed that the unusual gurney had no wheels.

The lead female discretely touched another icon, and Ronnie woke up. Circled around her bed was a group of men and women that she considered to be the best nursing staff on the planet, not to mention that several of them had become her dearest friends. It was very hard for Ronnie to leave them knowing that later they would be told that she had died on her way to the base hospital. The only consolation for the deception was the very real possibility that it could become true. If she did survive the transfer and be regenerated as Roy had told her, Ronnie knew that no one in the mainstream population of Earth could ever know.

There had been lots of hugs, hand holding, sweet murmurings, and even a few tears. Ronnie was sad to go but was also very hopeful. She knew that if what Roy had told her was true, and she was confident that it was, it was the only chance for life that she had. All she had to do was survive the next few hours.

Immediately after entering the service elevator, Roy leaned over Ronnie's bed, reassured her that all would be well, kissed her on the cheek, and took her by the hand. The lead female touched another icon on the mysterious electronic device causing Ronnie to slip back into an induced state of sleep.

There was a light rain falling when Ronnie, Roy, and the extraction team reached the roof. The lead female touched another icon on the device and an invisible force "bubble" formed around the entourage. Roy chuckled as he observed the raindrops trickling down the sides of the invisible umbrella.

"You guys have all the bases covered, don't you?"

The lead female offered a nod and a slight smile as she continued toward the waiting helicopter. Roy thought that it was quite odd that the blades weren't already spinning in preparation for takeoff, and, for that matter, the turbines weren't even running. Knowing Ronnie's condition and the urgency of the extraction, he couldn't understand how this could happen. He looked over at the lead female and asked why the chopper wasn't ready for takeoff. She just smiled again. Although the exterior of the aircraft looked for all intents and purposes to be a regular modern rescue helicopter, it was far from being conventional.

The two male attendants smoothly eased the floating gurney through the open bay door in the side of the helicopter and secured it into place. Roy hopped up into the helicopter with the lead female, leaving the two male and the other female attendant on the hospital helipad. No sooner than the doors were closed the rotors began to spin, and within seconds they were airborne. The silence and smoothness of the aircraft was extraordinary. At first, Roy had thought the chopper was one of the Visitors little ships made to look man-made, but, after looking around the craft, he discovered that, although there was a great deal of alien influence in the design, it was most definitely built on Earth for Earth. Roy couldn't figure out what the chopper's power source was but discovering that the aircraft was pilotless nearly took his breath away. They were traveling in what was essentially an unmanned drone.

The helicopter headed not to the base hospital as they had told the nursing staff but rather northwest over the Mohave Desert toward Area 51.

The lead female explained to Roy several reasons why they were flying in the Super Chopper, as he soon nicknamed it, instead of one of the small spacecraft. The two main reasons were plausible deniability and safety. Plausible deniability - the official story to cover up why Ronnie went missing (the chopper was off course and crashed in the desert with no survivors). Safety - the Jell used in all of the ships slowed all of the body functions to near zero, and the Visitors were concerned that Ronnie's heart might not restart. Also, flying in one of their ships without the safety of the Jell could tear a fragile human body apart.

Roy was listening intently when he realized how quiet the Super Chopper's cabin really was. There was no need to use headsets to communicate. It was just another odd thing among thousands of odd things that he had discovered since his journey with the aliens began three decades ago.

The workings of the human body were something that the extraterrestrials understood very well. Actually, they understood more about us than we understood ourselves. During the 30 plus years that Roy was aboard the interstellar exploration ships, the subject of human anatomy only came up once. With the aliens, the most direct answer was always their best and only answer. They were always very careful not to say or do anything that might overwhelm the fragile human psyche. Roy knew to accept their answer and the philosophy behind it. When asked about their vast knowledge of a race of people that they had only recently come into contact with (less than a century) they simply and unapologetically told him, "The Creator told us."

The Super Chopper flew through the darkness at normal operating speeds until they passed over the staged crash site (50 miles from the hospital) then began flying below Radar at twice the speed of the military's fastest helicopter attack ship.

An hour into the flight (about half way to Area 51), Ronnie's heart began to fall into arrhythmias. Roy watched helplessly as Ronnie's body was jolted three different times in a space of five minutes by her implanted defibrillator, causing her to stiffen violently then go limp like a rag doll. The arrhythmias had corrected to normal rhythms then once again had fallen into cardiac chaos.

The lead female had been monitoring her condition since she disconnected the support systems in the hospital room but no amount of preparation or medical procedures can accurately predict what the human body will do. Roy looked into his dying wife's face; she was deathly pale and no longer breathing.

"Do something!!! She's dying!!! Please do something!!!"

The lead female could see on her electronic device that Ronnie's heart had stopped. She pulled what appeared to be a hypodermic syringe from a pouch that was slung over her right shoulder and, after uncapping and evacuating it, quickly drove the needle into Ronnie's chest.

"One! Two! Three! Four! Five! Six! Seven! Eight! Nine! Ten!!!!"

Methodically scrolling through the icons on her devices screen, she touched one that looked like a heart with a lightning bolt running through it, causing Ronnie's implanted defibrillator to discharge one more time. Ronnie's body once again stiffened and then relaxed. Drawing a deep breath, she began to color up, and her respiration became semi-normal.

"We have rhythm!!! It's weak, but it's there!!"

"Hold on, Ronnie! We are just about there!!!"

Roy was sobbing and holding fast to Ronnie's hand as they flew swiftly through the night sky. Ronnie was unconscious and very weak when the chopper made its approach to Area 51.

***

Abduction?

It had been dark for just minutes, but the darkness and silence were closing in like a blanket. The feeling was suffocating. Why didn't the backup generator kick on? What had happened to the battery backup system? It was pitch black inside the facility and out. Even her trusty flashlight wouldn't work.

Sylvia sat frozen in her station computer chair, overtaken with fear and anxiety, unable to move or speak. It felt as if time itself had stopped. She couldn't tell if it had been 10 seconds or 10 hours since the power went off. Sylvia sensed that something extraordinary was occurring, but what?

Then suddenly there was an eerie glow in the room that seemed to be hanging in the air like smoke. Silently gliding out of the darkness, four apparitions moved into her peripheral vision. Unobtrusively surrounding her, the diminutive "beings" were about the size of a seven or eight year old human child, whitish gray in color, with large dark pupil-less eyes. They stood there silently, appearing to beckon to her to follow them with their odd looking little hands.

"Don't be afraid, Sylvie."

Was the voice coming from the darkness or was it inside her head? Sylvia wasn't entirely sure, but she was amazed that she wasn't terrified. Not only was she not terrified, but she felt amazingly calm. Sylvia had seen these creatures before but where? A very odd feeling of Deja vu over took her.

The voice was familiar. "Could it be?" Nobody else ever called her Sylvie, not even her mother.

"Don't be afraid, Sylvie. Go with my little Friends. I will explain everything soon."

How had they gotten into the bunker? Sylvia stood to her feet without even thinking, as if she was in some kind of dream state or hypnotic trance. All that Sylvia was sure of, when the little beings took her by the hand, was that this was nothing like she had ever experienced before or could have ever imagined. She walked hand in hand with the little creatures through the now wide open, "impenetrable" blast doors, down the runway toward a waiting shuttle ship that was hovering a couple of feet above the pavement. The cylindrical spacecraft was about 60 feet long and about 15 feet in diameter, tapering slightly to one end. The front and the back ends of the vehicle (Sylvia couldn't tell which was which) were spherical with no apparent cockpit or windows. The skin of the oddly shaped conveyance was covered with evenly spaced blisters about three inches in diameter, giving it a lumpy appearance. The entire ship was decorated in dark flat green except for a slight yellowing at the larger end.

Sylvia paused before reaching the shuttle, just to have a closer look at the fantastic contrivance and started laughing.

"Only Dad would send a flying pickle to pick me up!"

The humor of the moment was lost on the little ones accompanying her, but their experience with humans had taught them to "just go with the flow," as Roy often told them.

Leading her to the interior of the ship, Sylvia was placed into what at first looked like an elongated bowl filled to the edge with a substance resembling clear gelatin. As the substance totally engulfed her, Sylvia discovered that she was not breathing, and, for that matter; she wasn't sure if her heart was even beating. Quickly and unexplainably acclimating to her new surroundings, the scientist in her began analyzing her situation. The view from her pod or the "bathtub filled with goo," as she initially called it, was crystal clear allowing Sylvia to see in all directions at once, as if she then had a thousand eyes.

The ship quickly accelerated and began traveling at tremendous speed, although inside her pod she felt no movement at all. Sylvia was dumbfounded when the craft gently slowed to a stop on the backside of the moon.

She thought, "They were apparently waiting for something, but what?"

After the initial shock and adrenalin rush began to wear off, Sylvia began to look around the small craft that had just taken her (in mere seconds) from her temporary home in the Alaskan wilderness to the dark side of the Moon.

The interior of the ship was dimly lit, with a pale yellow glow that seemed to emanate from the superstructure itself. There were no specific compartments to the ship, no doors, or hatches, just areas formed like "bubbles." From the bubble that formed the passenger area, she could see the two little ones, who were apparently the pilots of the amazing machine, if it could in fact be called a machine. As Sylvia continued to make a visual inspection, she came to the realization that there weren't any moving parts to the ship. Whatever was propelling the craft at greater than hypersonic speeds was technology beyond anything ever imagined on her world.

Sylvia's thoughts turned back to the question, "What were they waiting for? Why were they hiding behind the moon?" Although she didn't understand, Sylvia was thoroughly enjoying the view of the Moon from her pod. It was a rare gift that few on Earth would ever have the opportunity to enjoy, and somehow she knew that a gift was exactly what it was.

As her curiosity peaked, overcoming her subsiding fear, she noticed a display that seemed to float midair in front of the little pilot on the left, who was watching it intently. On the display that looked like it was projected on a curtain of super fine diamond dust, was something that she was very familiar with - a volcano, but not just any volcano. It was Toby's volcano.

Almost overcome by the brilliance and detail of the display, Sylvia couldn't help but be green with envy. She couldn't help but think of the lives that could be saved with just this one small piece of the vast technological miracles possessed by this race of tiny intellectual titans.

***

Rumblings

Doctor Tobias Smith had spent most of the night monitoring the seismograph and G.P.S. readings. The mountain had gone eerily silent in the middle of the night so he had decided to get some rest. After taking one last look at his instruments, Toby leaned back in his camp chair, brushed his overgrown blond hair out of his face with his fingers, refocused his hazel eyes on the night sky, and yawned loudly, temporarily silencing the tiny tree frogs that seemed to be everywhere on the island. There wasn't a cloud in the sky, and the billions of stars were twinkling in the vast blackness of space, as if to remind us how alone mankind was in the universe. From the vantage point afforded him on this windswept escarpment, he could make out many constellations not viewable in other parts of the world due to the increasing light pollution. The continued growth of "civilized society" and an ever increasing desire for illumination just simply washes out the darkness.

The rest of the research team had decided to head down the winding A.T.V. trail through the jungle yesterday morning to meet the supply boat at the small abandoned fishing camp on the edge of island's only cove about three miles away, so Toby was alone. Despite the urgings of his research team to join them in what usually turned into a party, he had a feeling that things were about to get interesting, and he didn't want to miss a second of it. Toby wasn't delusional or naive to the fact that volcanoes can't be predicted with any degree of accuracy. An eruption could be eminent, or it may not occur ever again, but a gut feeling was a gut feeling. Toby found himself nodding off in his chair, so he groggily made his way into his tent and flopped down on his cot. In seconds, he fell fast asleep.

"Toby!"

He awoke from his short nap with a start as if someone had called out his name. The young volcanologist hurriedly crawled out of the mosquito netting covering his cot and jumped to his feet. Toby quickly checked his boots for unwanted visitors such as poisonous bugs and even snakes that were known to take refuge during the night, shaking them vigorously. He didn't want any complications this late in the game. Besides major medical help was days away. After pulling and lacing his boots, Toby began running from the door of his tent to the forward observation area nearly a half mile away.

Still panting from the uphill sprint to his observation platform on a ridge of volcanic rock, Toby stood on the precipice at the opposite end of the island from the crater mount. From this vantage point, he was able to see nearly all of the island.

The sun steadily rose to the southeast of the island, flashing off of the great expanse of open ocean that lay between the island and the Indonesian chain. Toby stood silently, taking in the sheer beauty of his surroundings. It almost took his breath away. He hoped to never be jaded enough to not be thrilled by how short and beautiful the sun's rising and setting were near the equator. From the windward side of the island, he could smell the millions of tropical flowers that were waving in the gentle ocean breeze, tainted only slightly by the sulfur seeping out of the volcanic fissures that had been widening over the last week. The thousands of exotic birds that had greeted him every morning since his arrival on the island four months ago were strangely silent this morning.

The mountain began to rumble again, and flocks of birds could be seen fleeing the impending eruption. The ancient volcano was reaching critical mass and could erupt at any moment. Bats that had spent the night devouring bugs of all kinds in the jungle below fluttered about aimlessly, too afraid to return to their lairs in the myriad of caves and vent tubes formed by past eruptions. He knew that the prediction of times and magnitude for volcanic eruptions were practically impossible. All anyone could do was watch and wait and hope that you could get out in time. Toby never was one to cut and run. He had to do the science because above the danger was always the science. What could be learned now could save lives later.

Toby had been in close contact with Sylvia for the last three days monitoring the mountain. If successful, it would be the first time ever to see an eruption from space. The pure data to be collected would be staggering. Sylvia had called earlier and warned him to get off the island, but now the satellite phone was dead.

***

Sylvia could see from the display that the volcano was quickly building pressure. The view from the ship extended deep within the Earth's crust, and she could tell from her limited knowledge of mantle mechanics that it was soon to reach critical mass. Terror quickly engulfed her when she noticed what looked like a bar graph in the upper edge of the display. They were timing the eruption, and her brother was on that ticking time bomb. Sylvia's mind was again racing. "What were they waiting for? Did they know that Toby was there?"

Just when the anxiety began to boil over into anger and Sylvia was just about to scream for help, the ship exploded out of its hiding place and flashed toward Earth.

***

Without any warning, the volcano exploded, shaking the ground so hard that Toby was knocked to the ground, scraping his shirtless back on the volcanic outcropping. He was laying there in amazement as he watched millions of cubic yards of dirt and rock being propelled skyward.

A voice on his hand radio was screaming for Dr. Smith to evacuate as soon as possible, but he knew it was too late to run. Toby was mesmerized by the advancing pyroclastic flow. The mountain had blown out the opposite side than was expected, and although he was three miles away, the superheated gas and rock would be there in mere minutes. Even with Sylvia's help, he wouldn't be able to escape.

The young explorer scientist had few regrets, but he did wish that he could have spent more time with his family and had the chance to say goodbye. As he regained his footing, Toby stood there and laughed to himself thinking, "I guess I won't find you now, Dad!"

***

Are you bored now?

The research team was still sleeping in their hammocks when the volcano roared to life. The force of the explosion blew the thatched roofs completely off the dormitory shacks.

Jim Friend struggled to get out of his swinging bed and fell to the ground in the process.

"What was that, Jim?"

Jim, Connie, and the rest of the team franticly ran out of the grass huts that they had used for a dormitory and stared with disbelief at the plume of smoke and ash rising with terrifying speed at the other end of the island. A pyroclastic flow was quickly closing the distance on the research camp some three miles to the west. The very camp that they would have all been in, if it had not been for the delayed arrival of the supply ship.

"Why is this happening??? This wasn't supposed to happen!!!!! Dr. Smith said there wasn't any danger, Jim!!!!!!"

Jim, with his years of leadership, sprang into action. The mild mannered draftsman started barking orders like a Marine drill sergeant.

"Run for the boat!!!!!!!!!!!! Run for the boat!!!!!!!!!!!! It's our only chance!!!! Drop everything and run for the boat now!!!!!!!!!!!"

The terrified collection of chaperones, researchers, and students frantically started running across the beach to the boat. Jim looked over his shoulder just in time to see chunks of flaming rock falling like hail on the main part of the island. Before they reached the half way point to the boat, a small herd of terrified wild feral hogs came running out of the jungle, trying to escape the coming cataclysm. A huge boar with four inch tusks nearly ran down Sito, who had momentarily paused to take a picture. No one saw him as he instinctively leaped nearly six feet into the air to avoid the beast. Undeterred, the squealing hog quickly passed Jim and Connie on its way to the water.

"There's your hog! Are you bored now?"

Jim, who was now running hand and hand with Connie, glanced over his shoulder and yelled.

"Rats!!!!"

"Rats? What is your problem?"

"Rats!!!"

Thousands of huge black rats and tiny mice that had been secretly living there lives in the undergrowth and rocks instinctively returned to the location where their ancestors came ashore from a merchant sailing ship that went down in a storm near the island. They came like a wave onto the beach, franticly trying to avoid certain death.

Dolly, Chase, and Angel were running hard for the dock when the rats caught up to them. Angel immediately began screaming at the top of her lungs, although the horror of the stampeding rats only made her run faster. Dolly on the other hand had grown up around woodland creatures of all sorts and on occasion had been involved in "rat killins" (as called by the locals from her area), an event when local farmers would gather together to surround and kill the thousands of rats and mice infesting their grain storage barns. She was unshaken by the waves of fleeing rodents, but, in empathy for Angel, she stayed close by her side. Chase was first to the boat and franticly started removing the orange foul weather tarpaulin cover, followed shortly by Angel and Dolly.

Jim looked back toward the now destroyed grass huts and spotted Feonia lying motionless in a crumpled heap on the beach. He started to return for her when Junior ran to her aid. Apparently she had also hesitated to take a photo when she was blindsided by a huge sow, flipping her into the air, and knocking her unconscious. Fortunately for Feonia, Junior had been taking a run along the beach when the eruption occurred. He saw her fall and was able to snatch her up and carry her to the boat before any more harm could come to her.

Nearly outpacing the hogs and running humans, the rats funneled onto the narrow wooden dock on the heels of the research team. The runners scrambled into the boat and got underway just as the fire hail reached their side of the island. As they cut the mooring ropes and slammed the throttle to full, hundreds of rats and mice scurried into the boat, overrunning the passengers, and creating total chaos.

The boat was nearly flying through the waves as a huge flaming boulder slammed into the dormitory shacks that minutes before had been their temporary home. It was an almost indescribable scene - a boat load of screaming and yelling people hanging on for dear life while simultaneously grabbing rodents by their tails and throwing them overboard. It was something that they would talk about for years. Nearly everyone and a few rats and mice hiding in the storage compartment of the boat had escaped with their lives. The rest of the animals didn't fare as well. As on cue, the sharks that infested the area around the island converged on the scene, snatching up mouthfuls of swimming rats, and taking great chunks of flesh out of the squealing hogs, turning the clear water of the cove a murky red. Luckily, the boat was too far out by then to witness the mayhem. Jim grabbed the two way radio and franticly tried calling Toby.

"Doctor Smith!!! Doctor Smith!!! Are you there?"

There was no answer. The fact that they had escaped with their lives was little consolation for the loss of their beloved leader. Connie and some of the others began weeping uncontrollably at the acknowledgement that they would never see Doctor Tobias Smith again.

Jim calmly reached for the ship to shore radio hoping to contact a ship in the area. They were too far from any other land to make it in such a small boat. For now, their main objective was to put enough distance between them and the island and to avoid the flaming hail that could easily sink their tiny boat.

"Mayday!!!! Mayday!!!! This is the research launch, Argo. Mayday!!!! Mayday!!!!"

As the boat hopped from wave to wave, the harried refugees looked back at what was left of the island that they had learned to love. Ash was already beginning to fall and obscure the destruction. Flame and smoke intermingled with lightning illuminated an unrecognizable landscape. The once majestic mountain that towered above the lush paradise was now a jagged pile of smoking rubble, half its original height.

Fourteen hours later the supply ship Neptune's Girlfriend, that had been slowly making its way back to its home port and had turned around when Jim issued a Mayday call, rescued the weary adventurers.

"Well, Connie, what do you want to do now?"

***

The Chase

The four trainee fighter jets peeled off one by one and headed back to the base. The instrument training was done for tonight. The rookie pilots would soon be ready for their instruments only flight examination.

After kicking the afterburners off and leveling out, Brad checked in with base. He was pleased to hear that the Smurflings had all survived the night's training. Following an hour of "coasting," he vectored south along the east side of the Sierra Nevada Mountains. Brad loved seeing Death Valley in the moon light. The whole area was a microcosm of nature; the topography ranged from mountains, to desert, to plains, to sand dunes, and lakes. He was always amazed to see huge pines, cactus, and even palm trees, scattered throughout the valley. Perplexing at best were the locations where he spotted camp fires in the expanse of the park. The question was always, "How on Earth did they get there!" The curiosity and bravery of man still, at times, shocked him.

Night maneuvers were always a challenge that he looked forward to, but, with his mother being in a terminal condition, it was hard being gone most every night. It would be nice if his brother and sister were able to be here with her. Brad hoped that the email had gotten to Sylvia in time for her to catch the next flight out. He didn't know exactly where Toby was at the time, but he knew that Sylvia always did. Toby was always off on some adventure or assignment with the geological survey.

In his spare time, which was rare, Brad was deeply interested in flight history. In his research through the archives of his local library, he had come across several articles about women flyers in World War II. One story in particular had intrigued him - Mary Smith. Smith! Brad had been instantly interested. Mary was the youngest of seven girls born to a rural farming family in northern Indiana, the only child in the Smith's history to ever go to college and the only one of her siblings to travel outside of their county. When the war broke out, she was in her second year of City College. Even with a degree, there were few opportunities for the women of that day, so she did a most extraordinary thing. She dressed like a man and hitchhiked to Texas.

Once there, she applied and was accepted for pilot training. After only six months of intensive flight training, Mary had been assigned to the Women's Air Force Service Pilots in the Spring of 1943. After two months of ferrying fighter planes and bombers to bases around the continental United States, she took an assignment to fly a P51 mustang from the aircraft plant in Dallas to an air base in California with a group of W.A.S.Ps., the same base that Brad was assigned to. After the second fuel stop, the fighter group encountered a thick cloud bank somewhere over Nevada. All of the aircraft emerged from the clouds except one. The air group searched the desert as long as they could, nearly running out of fuel and crashing themselves. There were several searches made of the suspected crash area, but no wreckage was ever found. Mary was lost and presumed dead.

If a young man could fall in love with a historical personality decades older than himself, then Brad most certainly did. Why Mary? That was a question on the minds of many admiring women. The truth was pure and simple - Mary was safe. She would never leave him, and she would never bother him.

Brad was deep in thought when a proximity alarm went off in the cockpit. His mind sprang into action, shaking him out of his complacency. He did a barrel roll to the right, down and away from the object that he had barely avoided. His mind was racing. What was that? Where did it come from? For that matter, where did it go? The object hadn't shown up on any of his instruments, radar, infrared, nothing, and was apparently traveling at incredible velocity. Brad quickly keyed up his headset microphone to check with ground control. There was no signal. How could there be no signal? There it was again, this time ahead of him. Brad throttled up on an intercept course. The thing in front of him was beautiful, mesmerizingly beautiful. It appeared to be disk shaped, like something you would see in an old science fiction movie. It was one of the coolest things that Brad had ever seen. Sometimes it was the color and appearance of polished aluminum, and then, instantly, it would change to a myriad of other colors and patterns within those colors.

The Rescue

The small ship began moving again out from behind the moon and into Earth's atmosphere at the dark side of the South Pole. Plunging into the icy water without so much as a splash, they quickly headed toward the southern tropical zone. The craft was flying through the depths of the ocean as though they were driving down Main Street. Sylvia couldn't help but be in envy of the mapping and navigational abilities these little creatures possessed.

As they surfaced and rose into the smoke of the erupting volcano, the ash and rock seemed to simply move out of the ships way as it dove down through the middle of the pyroclastic flow. Sylvia immediately knew where they were. She had been monitoring this area for months.

Toby was standing in amazement and fear of nature's power when the ship exploded out of the inferno. In the blink of an eye, he was lifted off the mountaintop and drawn into the ship by an ultra bright beam of light. This was not to be confused with a particle beam transporter that disassembles an object's atomic structure and then reassembles it in another location, as romanticized by many of Earth's science fiction writers, but was a much simpler and safer transport method. The beam actually was an extension of the flight bubble, formed into a tube-like configuration, that could be aimed with extreme accuracy and speed to engulf any object desired, no matter how large or small, depending only on the size of the ship. The object would then be pulled up the tube into the ship like sucking soda up a straw. If the action of the transporter could be slowed to a visible speed, the process would look similar to a python swallowing a rabbit. The beam worked the same way the flight bubble did by squeezing closed on one end and opening on the other making the process ultra fast and efficient. The transport beam could also be reversed for placing objects anywhere desired. Acceleration and deceleration were a moot point, as with the flight bubble, leaving any transported object completely unharmed and decontaminated.

As Toby arrived at the ship that by then was clear of the flaming inferno, he was still emitting a subconscious primal scream. Sylvia, with tears streaming down her face, laughed and hooted for joy as she saw their latest passenger. Out of the corner of her eye, Sylvia could see the little pilots look at her and Toby, then at each other. They were smiling and making the oddest chirping sound that she had ever heard.

Toby got settled into his pod, as the ship plunged back into the ocean and quickly made its way back to their entry point on the darkened side of Antarctica. Flying through the ocean at thousands of miles per hour, the siblings fell into awestruck silence. The look on Toby and Sylvia's faces was an expression of pure joy. They had no idea why or how it was all happening, but they couldn't wait to see what was next. Within what seemed like seconds, the craft had left the smoking inferno and the icy depths behind, once again shooting spaceward.

"Did you like the tour, Sylvie? I didn't want them to pull Toby out too soon," announced a familiar voice that seemed to come from everywhere at once.

Toby looked around the ship for the source of the voice but quickly discovered that the only other human onboard was Sylvia.

"Who was that?"

"Are you hearing voices, big brother?" Sylvia chuckled.

"Maaaaybeeee! Really, who was that?"

"I think it's our dear old dad."

"Really, you might be right, only Dad would think to pick us up...."

Toby and Sylvia smiled at each other and laughed while saying in unison, "...in a flying pickle!!!"

***

Who captured who?

Colonel Brad had been following the unknown object for the better part of an hour. He was so transfixed on the chase that he had lost track of everything else. It was as though he was having a dream.

Suddenly there was another warning light; this time it was low fuel. The buzzer shook him out of his dream state. Brad was having trouble contemplating how he could be losing his grip on concentration and reality. Was there a lack of oxygen? Had high altitude hypoxia set in? Was he blacking out for some other unknown reason? Was the ship in front of him performing some kind of hypnotic mind control or was he simply losing his grip on sanity?

Where was he? He wasn't over the mountains anymore. Brad had never punched out before, although he was well trained in the procedure. He hated the thought of losing such a beautiful aircraft, not to mention the 30,000,000 dollar price tag, but he knew it was either punch out or go down with the ship. How could he have let this happen? Grabbing the ejection handle, he prepared himself for the exhilaration and pure terror of what might possibly be the last moments of his life. "Nothing!!!"

Brad pulled the handle again. Again nothing happened. The engines flamed out and quickly went silent. He would have to try to land, but where? As he tried to scan the landscape below for a possible landing site, he couldn't see anything but the stars above and the object ahead of him.

Nestled safely in the spacecraft's invisible grasp, Brad began franticly trying to keep control of the fighter. Wait! Not only was the aircraft not losing altitude and airspeed, it was actually speeding up and gaining altitude!

Mach 1 with the engines silenced, he expected to hear the sonic boom caused by passing the sound barrier. Mach 2! Mach 3! Mach 4! Mach 5! These speeds were impossible for this aircraft. Brad was trying to rely on his years of training, but there was nothing in the flight manual about this. He tried the ejection seat again. When nothing happened, despite all that he knew about the machine he was careening across the sky in, Brad started to panic. He had to face it; he was trapped.

***

"Stand down, Colonel. We have this."

A great calm came over Brad. The voice was very familiar, someone out of his past, but who? Other questions were swirling in his mind. What was the object that was apparently towing him? Where were they going? This, as far as he knew, was the most extraordinary encounter ever witnessed by man. Why him?

"Who are you? Where am I? Where am I going?"

"All of your questions will be answered shortly, Brad!"

"Brad!! I am Colonel Bradford R. Smith of the United States Air Force!"

"Yes! Yes you are sir!"

Roy had spent the last thirty years thinking of his children as just that, children. The reality that they really were adults hit him hard in a way that the images onboard Mothership couldn't prepare him for. A wave of sorrow, loss and regret swept over him. Roy forced back the tears. He had a task to perform and the night was far from over.

Brad could see the lights of an airport in the distance nestled into the surrounding mountains. It was the strangest feeling to be coming in on approach to an unknown tarmac, at well above safe landing speed, with no power and no controls. Reaching the middle of the huge runway, Brad's fighter stopped in mid air and began to slowly descend vertically, until softly touching down. Where did it go? Brad sat in his cockpit trembling and franticly scanning the sky. A figure approached from the darkness and silently motioned for him to deplane and follow. Toby and Sylvia had been gently deposited on the silent tarmac just moments before, and the saucer shaped shuttle had immediately shot skyward and out of sight.

Chapter 6
Vindication

Brad crawled out of the cockpit and slid off of the wing to the tarmac. He cautiously followed the shadowy figure toward a waiting group of people standing in the glow of a hanger light. He quickly recognized his siblings and ran the last few yards to their position. He grabbed Sylvia and then Toby, giving them a bear hug. Toby realized at that point that not only was he and Sylvia wearing some sort of ultra light one piece jump suits, the abrasions on his back were completely gone. Brad, Toby, and Sylvia were still hugging and chattering when a young, sharply dressed woman approached them.

"Welcome to Area 51 Madam, Sir, Colonel. Please follow me to the briefing room. All of your questions will soon be answered. Colonel, if you wish to change, we have uniforms available."

Brad, Toby, and Sylvia silently followed the young woman off the tarmac to a small utilitarian office in the front section of a huge empty aircraft hangar. Brad scanned the young woman from head to toe, not in a prurient way but in an attempt to ascertain her rank and branch of service. He was surprised that her uniform contained elements of all the branches of service and no insignia other than a small American flag over the right breast pocket. Brad took advantage of the offer to change out of his flight suit and quickly changed into a uniform that he wasn't familiar with. At that point he really didn't care what he was wearing. His siblings didn't say anything, but he looked to them like a 1950s gas station attendant.

Their minds were such a jumble of thoughts and emotions that they couldn't talk, even to each other. What did she mean? "All your questions will be answered." The thousands of questions generated in the last few hours alone would take a lifetime to decipher.

"Our apologies, Director Kenny was supposed to be present at your arrival, but he is on an Elk hunting trip in the Northern Rocky Mountains, and we couldn't contact him. Normally, we would wait for his return, but time is a luxury that we just don't have. He will be greatly disappointed that he missed all of this. Please take a seat."

The entire room began to vibrate ever so slightly as the huge office/elevator began to make its decent. Picking up speed by the second, they were unaware of how deep into the underground complex they had been taken. The elevator slowed to a stop on the 75th level, some 450 feet below the level of the hanger floor above. The room began to move horizontally for several seconds and then slowed to a stop. The wall in front of them slid to the side revealing a small but comfortable viewing room. A middle aged male officer, wearing a very similar but more masculine uniform as the young woman was wearing, stepped into and then to the side of the main isle.

"Please come in and have a seat in the front please. In a few moments, all of your questions will be answered."

There it was again. "All your questions will be answered." What questions? There were so many questions. How could these people possibly answer all of their questions?

The siblings took their seats and then settled in for what they expected to be a long detailed briefing. As the lights were lowered, a strange looking device rose from the floor. The device looked similar to a human eye, about the size of a basketball, but with no visible cornea. It just hovered there with no visible means of support. The object was so strangely attractive that they couldn't take their eyes off of it for even a second.

Peering into the blackness of the device's lens, they suddenly became aware of what must have been millions of sounds and images pouring into their minds like water flowing from a dam that had broken.

Now they understood why. Now they understood why it had to be done this way. All of those years of wondering where their father had gone, all of the sorrow, hurt, and anger were explained and obliterated in a millisecond. It was as if they had always known.

He had no choice, and, because he had no choice, the government had taken very good care of his family- from the California house that Ronnie had won in a raffle that she didn't remember entering located strategically close to the Air Force base, to the many mentors and educational advantages each of the children had afforded to them. Not to mention, the winnings from a lottery ticket that had miraculously stuck to Ronnie's car windshield just after winning the house, making the move to California not only possible but felt nearly mandatory. Ronnie had wanted desperately to get away from all the controversy and notoriety generated over the disappearance of her husband - the controversy and notoriety that were in a great part generated by the government to push the family into fleeing to California. Moving out of state would be a Godsend, so she changed their last names and dropped out of sight, or so she thought.

It was the least the world could do for the invaluable service that their father had performed for the last 30 years. Others had been meticulously trained for the role of an intergalactic ambassador but, when it came to choices, the Visitors wanted him!

***

The Search

It had been a short night, and Sam was still exhausted from the flight to Las Vegas and the two and one half hour drive to his two bedroom ranch style bungalow sitting in the foothills just off the Extraterrestrial Highway that ran past the entrance to Area 51. Sam Drocer lived alone and enjoyed cooking. When he was at his home in the desert he cooked most of his meals, but he did occasionally have breakfast at the Little A'Le'Inn café that was just down the highway from home. He was sitting in a booth by the window sipping his coffee, trying to wake up, when the first of several black S.U.V.'s sped by the little cafe in the desert. He jumped to his feet and ran to the door. Sam was right. They were heading for Area 51.

During the night, Sam had been awakened by what he believed to be a commercial airliner being escorted by at least four fighter jets, which he found a little odd but not totally unheard of in this part of the world. Despite his exhaustion that he knew was more than just travel fatigue, he had gotten up, loaded his Rokon Trailbreaker (a two wheel drive motorcycle sporting fuel and water tanks in the wheels and high flotation tractor type tires) on its trailer, pulled his camera gear out of his road car, and then packed his gear into his trusty old beat up four wheel drive Blazer, just in case. Sam had a feeling that something good was going to happen out in the desert, and he didn't want to miss it.

After breakfast at the little diner, he headed down the narrow highway toward his favorite surveillance location, Peek-a-boo Peak, the closest viewable location to Area 51. Sam had searched for years to get closer access to the area to no avail. Everywhere he had tried was locked down and guarded under penalty of deadly force. The spots that seemed accessible, upon closer inspection, were found to be under surveillance by closed circuit cameras, listening devices, motion detectors, roaming security personnel, and who knows what else. Years ago, there had been a vantage point on a peak much closer to the area, but the government expanded the borders and pushed everyone, including the most determined, completely off the reservation.

Just as Sam began slowing in preparation for the turn on to the desert trail, two unmarked windowless tour busses nearly collided with him, forcing his blazer off the highway into the ditch and nearly flipping the trailer and Rokon. After checking for damage, he gathered his wits about him, pulled the Blazer into 4-wheel drive, and continued on his way. It wasn't like this kind of thing hadn't happened before.

It was getting late when Sam finally reached the trail leading to the summit of Peek-a-boo Peak. He would have to hurry, if he was to reach his destination before dark. He had gone as far as possible with the old Blazer, so he stopped and unloaded the bike in preparation for the grueling six mile trek across the rocky scrub brush strewn hills to the only vantage point accessible to civilian eyes. Pulling his ragged old Army green backpack full of equipment and supplies to his shoulders, Sam jerked the starter rope on the aging but reliable Rokon. The two cycle engine sputtered to life, sounding more like an outboard boat motor than a motorcycle. He knew the capabilities of the old machine well, confident that it could take him just about anywhere and back. Sam, on occasion, had told curious onlookers that the trailbreaker was part motorcycle, part bulldozer, and part mountain goat. He was also fond of telling people that it would take you anywhere you wanted to go and some places you didn't.

Sam tightened the chin strap on his helmet and revved the engine a couple of times, making it cackle like a chainsaw.

Confident that all was in order, he dropped it into low gear and started out across the desert.

Sam was beginning to get another headache, so he stopped to take some medication in a futile attempt at slowing the advancing wave of pain and wondered to himself if chasing after phantoms was worth all the trouble. As he herded the Trailbreaker up the path, expertly balancing the awkward bike and the heavy backpack full of equipment, his mind was whirling. Was the tumor in his scull going to take his life before he could complete his life long search? Will the chemotherapy scheduled to start next week work? Would anyone care if he did die?

Sam was suddenly pulled away from a mental track that he really didn't need to go down anyway, when a fighter jet began circling slow and low above. Stopping in a small clearing at the side of the path, he wanted to catch his breath but, more importantly, he wanted the fighter pilot to get a good look at him. Sam was certain by now that the powers that be knew full well who he was, what he was up to, and found no threat in him. The pilot seemed satisfied with what he saw, and soon the plane disappeared as quickly as it had appeared.

Sam continued on the trail through the brambles and sagebrush, clawing his way up over shelf rock and loose gravel to the clearing on top, the old bike had once again proven itself faithful. Sam was still setting up his equipment and settling in for the night when an unmarked black helicopter came in for a closer look. After about ten minutes of super close fly by's and rotor wash generated dust storms, the chopper retreated, apparently satisfied that he was not going to be intimidated into leaving the remote peak. Now all he had to do was wait!

***

The smartly dressed young women stepped to the front of the room as the alien device disappeared back into the floor of the small conference room.

"If you are ready, we are needed topside."

By the time that the siblings reached the tarmac level, the base appeared to be deserted. Personnel, previously scrambling around like ants making last minute preparations and adjustments, were nowhere to be seen. There were no banks of sophisticated audio-visual equipment or crowds of specialists like they had seen in their implanted memories. In their absence, everything and everyone had been cleared from the area except one military medical helicopter and two attendants who were apparently offloading a patient. Brad, Sylvia, and Toby stood silently on the near empty tarmac wondering what was going to happen next.

Sitting silently in a darkened auditorium far beneath the tarmac, the President of the United States of America and several high ranking military and governmental officials watched the event of a lifetime unfold before them on a huge, high definition, closed circuit video wall.

After a few moments of contemplation, the siblings finally were able to communicate with each other.

"How is Mom doing, Brad?"

"She was stable when I saw her three hours ago. I really wish she could be here to see this!"

"Toby and I have been meaning to come home to see her. We both want to thank you for keeping us informed about her condition!"

"I want to go and see her as soon as we are done here. The project that was monopolizing all of my time and most of Sylvia's time literally blew up in our faces about two hours ago, so I am free to be with Mom as long as she needs me. Is she still at Mercy General?"

"Yes, Sir."

"Wow. At ease, Colonel Brad. I am moving home too. The main reason I was in the Arctic was to be awake all night and keep tabs on Toby the Terrible here."

"Okay. Okay. Old habits are hard to break. I am glad that you and Toby are going to move home. I'm very pleased that Dad is able to come home before it's too late."

"With all this technology, you would think that there would be something available to help Mom!"

***

Lock and Load

It had taken the better part of an hour to get the Bird loaded into the two ton delivery truck before they could finally get on the road. John and Carlos drove the truck while Popeye and Nikola followed close behind in a Hummer for security. This was the day that they had planned for over the last several years. Were they ready? They hoped so. The computer systems had been bench tested, and the engine on the Bird had been fired once before being installed. Everything from the guidance systems, to the wing deployment hardware, to the laser aiming lens, functioned perfectly, that is, on computer models. The laser and generating module also remained for all practical purposes untested.

The problem was not in lack of decision making, determination, or even funding and materials, but in time itself, actually, the lack of it. The W.D.C. and the splinter cell members fully expected to have several more years to prepare. According to their inside sources, They weren't due to return for several more years. Something had occurred to bring Them back early, but what? According to the agreement reached at the last Visitation, they would not enter Earth's proximity without prior notice, and then, only under extreme stealth conditions. To the most extreme members of the W.D.C., it could mean only one thing: WAR!!!

It was nearly noon when the clandestine convoy reached their turn off. The abandoned rock quarry located on the western edge of the Warren Peak's wilderness area was now within reach. Bought by the U.S. Forestry Service in 1982, the quarry was effectively just a large hole in the ground, secluded, defensible, and reasonably close to their pending target. Too short for even a small airplane to land on its flat bottom and too much wind turbulence for a helicopter, it was a perfect for hiding a large generator and mobile missile launch platform.

The trucks slowly pulled up to the locked gate that blocked the gravel road leading to the mouth of the quarry, nearly five miles away. The road, if you could call it that, wound around alongside a dry creek bed that was impassible during the rare gully washers that some years plagued the region. Sheltered by huge Ponderosa Pines, the road was nearly invisible from the air and almost impossible to negotiate when wet. The temperature was already in the mid seventies. The birds were chirping, the chipmunks and squirrels were playing, and there was a slight breeze wafting through the huge pines, filling the air with an aroma that stirred the hunter's soul in the soon to be world-saving "Heroes."

Carlos and his band of Heroes finally arrived at the huge metal gate at the entrance to the quarry. It had taken them over an hour and a half of creeping and bumping through washouts, ruts, and mud holes. At one point along the road, the cargo truck nearly rolled over after the creek bed crumbled and had to be winched back into position with the Hummer.

The four warriors crawled out of their vehicles and quickly pushed the large chain link and barbed wire gates to the side. The strange thing about the rock quarry was not only its location (too far from any structure to be used for building stone) but the fact that the whole place was surrounded by a ten foot high fence with barbed wire at the top. The main gate was supported by two massive concrete posts with brace walls running to the opening rock face of the quarry. It looked to the men to be either an abandoned gold mine or a small prison camp. Who really knew what its original purpose was? It met their needs to a tee.

As soon as the convoy came to a stop inside the quarry, it was time to unload and get set up. They were hoping that they still had some time but, at that point, how much time was the biggest concern. If they missed the window, the opportunity might not present itself again for a lifetime.

"Man, oh, man! I sure am glad that we tied the Bird down like we did! I knew it would be rough, but I didn't think it would be that bad, Carlos."

"What's up with the road, men? I thought you guys checked it when you came up and did a run out on the generators! What did you do all week, hang out at the pool?"

The quarry had a mostly flat bottom, with the exception of the far left corner. For some unknown reason, the men who performed the excavation, blasted out a pit several feet deep, about the size of a small swimming pool. Whatever it was originally designed for, the spring water that filled the pool, as cold as it was, really felt good on a hot Wyoming summer day.

"It was good last week. There must have been a gully washer or maybe Rambo there just can't drive!"

"Hey! You try herding this elephant down that rabbit trail!"

Carlos, being the oldest and most austere of the group, stepped around the corner of the delivery truck and, without a word, told them to shut up and get to work. Not having children of his own, although he would have made a fine father, Carlos had acquired "the look" from many years of dealing with young military personnel. It was like the look you got from your father when you were goofing around in church. He could put the fear of God into you from fifty feet away.

The men quickly leveled and secured the moving truck, using the custom built hydraulic leveling cylinders. The outriggers were only one of many unique features that would not be found on a normal moving truck.

Carlos revved the truck's engine and the seemingly generic moving van began to open up like some sort of gigantic Chinese puzzle box. The sides folded in half lengthwise and lowered to the ground, making a blast shield that protected the undercarriage and drive train of the launch platform. The roof section slid forward and rolled up like a large metal garage door, protecting the cab and engine compartment. The rear doors of the truck smoothly lowered to form a ramp/ blast shield while the electric servo motors on the launch platform groaned under the stress of the "bird" as it rose to its fully upright position. Gleaming in the afternoon sun, there stood what the Heroes believed to be the instrument that would save mankind from total annihilation. To them, it was an awe inspiring sight.

"Snap to it, gentlemen. Time is short! Make sure the R.A.T.O. (rocket assist take off) motors are mounted correctly. We don't want to die trying to save the world. We want to be heroes, not martyrs!"

Carlos was just following a hunch and hoping that the extraterrestrials would try to contact Barry. According to his inside source, there was a good chance that They would do just that. The problem with inside sources in a super secret society is that no one person knows everything, and there was a lot that his sources didn't know. Although Carlos didn't know that the entire Smith family would be onboard Their ship, it wouldn't have made a difference if he had because haters just have to hate.

Inside the cab of the cargo truck (now the command booth), Carlos was careful to not let the other men see his laptop computer monitor as he tracked Barry's signal. There would be too many questions if they could see what he was seeing. The signal beacon had been moving at ground level for several hours but had been nearly stationary for the last hour on the top of Devil's Tower, Wyoming, less than 20 miles from the launch site.

***

Success at last

Sam Drocer sat silently on Peek-a-boo Peak, peering across the hilltops into the distant dry lake with a telephoto lens system that would have made most astronomers jealous. He was prepared for anything. If he couldn't catch the images that he wanted on camera or video, there was always infrared imaging or any number of electronic surveillance devices he had collected over the years.

There had been several aircraft land during the early evening, but it had been strangely quiet for the last couple of hours. Sam was just about to nod off in his camping chair when something caught his eye in the night sky. Out of the west, just above the horizon, he could barely make out a point of light, a very fast moving point of light.

Sam trained his equipment on the incoming object and started documenting its arrival. Could this be the event that he had hoped for most of his life? Could he finally stand up to the scientific community and declare the truth about extraterrestrial spacecraft and their Visitations to the Earth?

As the light grew nearer, he recognized the light configuration of a military aircraft. His heart sank, and he fell back into his camp chair. But wait! The fighter was chasing something, and, from his vantage point, he could tell that both objects were traveling several times faster than was possible for anything less than a rocket or hypersonic drone. There was no jet engine sound, no sonic boom.

Once again, he trained his equipment on the lights. The fighter slowed quickly and stopped over the middle of the runway. Sam was dumbfounded at seeing the aircraft descend vertically onto the tarmac. It definitely wasn't a jump jet. But what was it? And where did the other object go? Moments later something shot skyward and out of sight. Sam knew in his gut that this wasn't over yet!

Within the space of about 20 minutes, another set of lights appeared, this time out of the southwest, just above the horizon moving much slower than the ones previously but still moving at a good clip. That set of lights also slowed toward the middle of the tarmac and descended vertically. Sam was puzzled. This time the aircraft appeared to be some sort of military medical evacuation helicopter, but it had been flying way too fast and way to quietly.

"What on Earth is going on?"

Sam was double-checking his equipment, insuring that everything was operating correctly, when several other small craft began approaching the base. They seemed to be coming from all quadrants. As his equipment whirred and beeped in the background, he began jumping around and shouting like a kid at Christmas time.

As the unknown craft approached the base, it looped and spiraled in what appeared to be some kind of Arial ballet.

Suddenly, during the display, another craft descended to the same spot where the military aircraft had landed, paused briefly on the ground, and then shot skyward. In a blink, it was out of sight, seemingly taking the other ships with it.

Sam collapsed in his camp chair exhausted. His mind was racing; he was going to be the most famous photographer in the world. He might even get the Nobel Prize for this!

***

The Arrival

Within minutes of the siblings return to the tarmac, a larger ship than the other seemed to just fall out of the sky. Coming to an abrupt stop just above their heads, they could feel the tingle of the unseen forces that propelled the sleek ship flowing around them. As a circular disk lowered from the bottom of the craft and silently contacted the pavement, the siblings stood in silence trying to comprehend what was taking place before their eyes. There was now an opening of about twenty feet in diameter in the bottom of the vessel. The soft glow of blue light was emitting from the interior. The ship was different than the one that had rescued Toby in that it had the classic flying saucer shape portrayed in many comic books and movies. The vehicle was everything that they had ever imagined a flying saucer to look like. It was about forty feet in diameter, with the appearance of polished aluminum and multicolored lights that seemed to emanate from the hull material itself, pulsating in a myriad of patterns.

"What do you think, kids? I designed it myself. I always did like the classics."

The siblings turned in the direction of the voice. While they had been distracted by the ships arrival, the two attendants standing by the medical chopper had apparently off loaded a patient and had joined them beneath the ship.

"We have to hurry. Your mother is gravely ill. She slipped into a coma on the helicopter flight, and, if They are going to save her life, our long awaited family reunion will have to wait."

As they all huddled around their dying wife and mother, Ronnie was levitated off the gurney and appeared to float into the hatch area of the ship, leaving the lead female attendant behind to return to the "Super Chopper." Before she turned to go, Roy made eye contact with her and gave her a thankful smile. Although no words were spoken verbally or telepathically, a strong feeling of respect and gratitude washed over her soul. The floor disk then raised the family up into the opening like an elevator but with no visible means of support. Once inside the ship, Ronnie was placed into a pod identical to the pods on the small ship that had rescued Toby and Sylvia.

Suddenly a bright white stream of light shot into Ronnie's pod and, in an instant, it removed the heart disease that had severely weakened her aging body. Ronnie opened her eyes and smiled at her long absent husband and three bewildered children. She knew from her late night visits with Roy that curing her terminal disease wouldn't be the end of the repair that was to be done. Not only was the advanced medical knowledge of these benevolent beings capable of curing all of the human diseases and ills, they could stop and reverse the ageing process almost indefinitely, causing the chosen subjects to live for hundreds of years.

One by one the newly reunited family took their places in the Jell pods. After they were secure in the soothing grip of the Jell, the pods were turned upright, making it possible for the family to communicate face to face, something that hadn't been possible for decades. Watching from their pods, they could see several of the small gray beings sitting in front of monitors that seemed to appear and disappear at will as if they were some sort of projection.

In their pods, they had complete freedom to communicate within their minds. They were all in complete agreement that they would live this adventure together. More than a second chance, it would be a new beginning.

"We have two more stops to make before we can start our lives over."

***

Otis couldn't believe his eyes. In the last two hours, the leaders of the world had come out in mass to meet with the Aliens. Apparently, government officials had somehow been in contact with Them for the last three decades. According to the news announcer, recently declassified papers had just been released to the media, outlining an agreement of sorts with "our new friends." Otis leaned back in his easy chair thinking about how everyone's life was about to change for the better.

***

The Encounter

Sam Drocer sat in his camping chair at the top of Peek-a-boo Peak exhausted from the events of the last few minutes. The pure ecstasy and joy he had experienced was almost more that he could handle in his weakened state. If he never got to document another UFO "Visitation" in his whole life, he could die happy.

Just when Sam thought he had seen it all, a larger, saucer-shaped ship seemed to appear out of nowhere, falling from the star studded sky at more than terminal velocity. Expecting it to crash into the distant air base, he was so startled that he almost fell out of his chair. Searching the area intently for what seemed like an eternity, he saw no sign of the ship. He knew that he had seen it fall, but there was no explosion or anything visible to any of his instruments. Then he realized that it must have soft-landed between the huge aircraft hangers. Within two or three minutes, the ship reappeared and began to regain altitude, slowly gliding silently across the hilltops toward his position.

Sam couldn't believe his luck! This was without a doubt the best day of his life! The saucer moved to within 50 feet of where he was now standing bolt upright, coming to a stop directly in front and above him.

There would be no doubt in the minds of the skeptical public, with the photos he was getting from this vantage point. Hovering directly in Sam's line of sight, the ship began pulsating with light and sound as if someone was showing off just for him. Sam busily documented as much of the amazing extraterrestrial spacecraft as he could. He didn't know when this extraordinary opportunity would end, and he wanted to get as much information as possible.

Suddenly an ultra bright beam of light emanated from the underside of the saucer shaped craft, lifting Sam from the ground a few feet and holding him perfectly still in its grip. In a millisecond, the cancer was removed from his body by the alien's medical beam. Unbeknownst to Sam, he was then placed into his camping chair, freed from the deadly disease that was destroying his brain.

The saucer silently and quickly pulled away from Peek-a-boo Peak traversing the 800 miles to Devils Tower in less than a minute. The whole family was silently beaming with pride at the profoundly caring and generous act of mercy that their newly found patriarch had shown toward Sam, a total stranger in need.

Yes but No

As Sergeant Bill slept fitfully in his custom built and armored motor home at the base of Devil's Tower, the other campers in the K.O.A. campground slept peacefully, having had no idea what kind of firepower lay concealed just feet away. The motor home was a mobile tracking station, bunker, and launch platform - home sweet home for Barry and Bill. If so much as a mosquito did anything unusual, the monitors would see it.

It was pitch black on the top of Devil's Tower, and the clouds were so thick that they obscured all light from above. Barry was beginning to wonder if he should have stayed on the summit or not. The weather report had given an all clear for nearly the whole state. Whatever was going to happen would just have to happen. It was suicide to try and climb down in the dark.

Barry tried his flashlight, but nothing happened, so he decided to ignite one of the emergency glow sticks that were part of his survival gear. Barry had never been afraid of the dark or much of anything else for that matter. Sergeant Bill was a real taskmaster when it came to self defense and physical fitness. Over the many years of training, Barry's 6' 2" body had acquired an impressive physique. Powerful biceps, rippled abs, small waist and the legs of a marathon runner, he cast an imposing silhouette. Topped with steely grey eyes, coal black hair and a military flat top, he was admired and feared.

As he cracked the glow stick's cylinder and shook it to life, the realization that he was not alone on The Tower startled him. Barry immediately called upon his battle training. Like a deer fawn in an unknown danger situation, he stayed perfectly still, analyzing the situation, trying to decide on the appropriate action. To act without thinking could be a fatal mistake. Thanks to the instinctive reaction that had been instilled in him by Bill through years of intensive training, he had acquired enough self-control to stay motionless for nearly an hour.

From the edge of the darkness came a calm voice.

"Barry, can I speak with you?"

There were many questions flying through Barry's mind. Who is this person? For that matter, was it a person or something else entirely? If it was a person, how did he get up on the top of the tower in the dark? What does he want? Is he a friend or an enemy?

"Barry, I have come to ask you a question."

Barry, recognizing Roy's voice, started feeling strangely at ease, relaxed enough to respond to the intruder.

"I know you. You're that guy on the road that almost ran over me when I was a kid."

"Yes, Barry. Sorry about that."

Barry sat there stunned; this man was the only link that he knew of to the ship and his little "Friends." Remembering back to his childhood, he knew that the last time they were together he had seen him leave with Them. The question on Barry's mind now was, "Why was he here now?"

"You said that you had a question to ask me?"

Roy stepped closer into the light. Barry could make out the form of a healthy, average height, young man in his early thirties. On closer inspection, Barry could tell that he wasn't dressed for the climb up from the forest floor to the summit. Roy was clad in a black, pocketless, zipperless, one piece jump suit that shimmered in the moonlight. In Barry's estimation, Roy wasn't dirty or sweaty, and there was no way that anyone could climb Devil's Tower without getting dirty and sweaty. And, for that matter; where was his gear? Barry was well aware of how dirty the climb up the volcanic walls could be. Although he loved the climb, he was really looking forward to a hot shower at base camp. Besides, Bill would have alerted him if someone was on the way up. How did he get here? He didn't just drop out of the sky, did he?

"Would you be willing to join me in a little adventure?"

"What kind of little adventure?"

"First, I have a gift of sorts for you. Then, you can decide."

Despite his training, Barry suddenly found himself standing erect. Every fiber of his being was at full alert. Slowly stepping out of the darkness were two of the small silver grey beings that he had searched for most of his life, coming to a stop, one on each side of Roy. Were they the benevolent, innocent, fun loving, Friends that he met as a boy, or were they the dangerous, devious, malevolent, invaders that Sergeant Bill told him they were? The next few moments would tell the tale.

Many young children have the intuitive ability to read the intentions of others, especially adults, and Barry trusted his little Friends then, so why would he not trust them now? The decision wasn't very hard to make. Barry always knew that if he had the opportunity to be with them again, he would jump at the chance. Collapsing back onto the ground in amazement and adrenal exhaustion, Barry saw that the two little beings were looking up at Roy, who quickly began to smile.

"What's up?"

"They want to know if they can speak directly to you. Their race feels that it is rude to speak into another's mind without permission. That is why they used a tonal vocabulary at the Visitation. That is also why they used the implanted vision that drew your mother and I to Devil's tower all those years ago."

"Oh, man! You bet!"

"We missed you, Barry."

Barry pulled himself together and lay there speechless although, at that point, his mouth was hanging wide open. The little beings held out what passed for arms, in a beckoning pose that they had learned was a gesture of friendship and openness. Although the greeting was acquired from the Earthlings that they had come into contact with during their earlier excursions to this planet, the affection was genuine.

Telling the Visitors apart on a physical level was very difficult because of the lack of distinguishable facial features, but being in mental contact with them made Barry realize that these two in particular were ones that he had gone to the ship with as a child.

Barry's mind was still awash with anxiety and exhilaration, but, despite the shock and correspondingly the adrenalin rush, he summoned the clarity of spirit to his mind and began to speak.

"I missed you too. I have been searching most of my life for you. Where have you been?"

"We would like to show you. We would like that very much."

"I told you earlier, Barry, that I had a question to ask you."

"Yes, a question?"

It was apparent to Roy that Barry was nearly overcome with emotion.

"Would you like to hear that question now?"

Barry snapped himself out of the emotional fog that had overtaken his mind.

"Yes, Sir."

"Consider your answer diligently but be aware that our time here is short. We will need an answer as soon as possible! The question is, "Would you like to come with us?"

Barry instinctively answered.

"Yes!! Definitely!! Yes!!!"

Suddenly he remembered Bill waiting patiently and loyally below in the motor home.

"How long would we be gone, Roy?"

"That would be hard to say, Barry. We are only here now because of extenuating circumstances. From here, our mission will eventually take us beyond the edge of this galaxy. Among others, we have come back for you, but only if you want to come. I want you to understand, it is totally your choice."

After a few moments contemplating the pros and cons, Barry came to a decision.

"I have dreamed about this, as I have told you, for most of my life. I have weighed my decision very carefully, but I am really sorry to tell you that my answer has to be no. As much as I want to go with you and explore the universe, I just can't be gone that long. There is a grumpy old man waiting for me down at the base of this tower that I just can't leave behind, and I am positive that he wouldn't come with us. He is the only father I have ever known, and my uncle and I are the only family that he has left. He dedicated his life to protecting Mom and me, and now I owe as much to him. I don't regret my decision one ounce, but, one day, I know that my circumstances will be different and, at that point, I would love to be able to go."

One of the creatures slowly stepped forward, stretched its little body to the same height as Barry's, who was by then standing, elongated its arms, and embraced him in the warmest hug that the young man had ever experienced.

"We will watch and listen. When it is time, we will send for you."

"Well, Barry, regretfully, our time is up. I am sorry that you can't come with us now, but I highly applaud your dedication to your family. He is lucky to have a son like you."

A wave of regret once again passed over Roy, and tears came to his eyes as he remembered leaving his family behind all those years ago. Melancholy quickly gave way to hope as he thought about the people he loved in the cloaked ship hovering directly above his position.

Roy looked down at his companions, chuckled out loud, then, with a huge smile, he turned to Barry.

"Catch you on the flip side!"

The two men shook hands and exchanged a manly bear hug.

"Later, dude!"

Barry laughed out loud, and, as quickly and silently as they came, Roy and the two aliens returned to the ship hiding in plain sight among the clouds.

***

Otis had been glued to his seat for what seemed to be all night long, only leaving to attend to the necessities of life. On the screen in front of him was unfolding the most extraordinary events that he had ever witnessed. The leaders of the world, including the President of the United States, were poised to meet with the leaders of the "peace ships," as the media was now calling them. It would be a worldwide simulcast, with as many as 50 views being posted on the one screen. Otis was very glad that he had made the decision to invest in a high definition flat screen instead of going a cheaper route.

***

A shot in the dark

It was pitch black in most of the quarry, except for the glow of a small campfire that Popeye had built to heat up some food and coffee. They all knew full well that it could be a long night of waiting, that is, if anything happened at all. Everything was ready. All of the components were connected and tested. The laser generator could be powered up at a moment's notice, and the "bird" could be airborne within minutes.

Carlos was wide awake and monitoring Barry's signal, but the other three men were either asleep or nearly there. By all accounts, it was a beautiful night. A myriad of stars were twinkling in the vast Wyoming sky. Other than the occasional call of a night bird, the night was dead silent.

Suddenly, something large, or at least it sounded that way, smashed into the fence that ran around the perimeter of the quarry. All four men jumped to their feet and peered into the darkness. Popeye immediately slipped on the night vision goggles that he always had with him, pulled his nine millimeter pistol from its holster, and ran into the darkness towards the unknown intruder or intruders.

"Wow! That guy is completely nuts!"

In the darkness, on the other side of the quarry, the sounds of conflict echoed off the rock walls. First, another crash against the fence and then a cry of pain were making the hair stand up on Carlos's neck. The men didn't know if they should run for cover or get ready to stand and fight. They certainly didn't expect to have to defend the operation, so Popeye was the only one that was packing firepower.

Suddenly, they could hear what sounded like a pack of dogs fighting, and a muffled squeal, then silence again. Listening intently to the darkness, they all jumped when the silence was broken by the familiar double tap report of a semiautomatic firearm, followed by the sound of footsteps heading back in their direction. Popeye emerged from the darkness with a smile on his face.

"Now we know what the fence is for!"

"What are you talking about? What on Earth did you shoot at? We thought the compound was under siege!"

"Nope! Just a couple of coyotes chasing a deer! They would have got him too, if I hadn't scared them off. It looks like the fence is there to keep hikers and wildlife from falling into the pit. You weren't spooked were you? Ha! You were!"

Before the other Heroes could try and defend themselves, Carlos was drawn back to his computer. Barry's signal was airborne and slowly moving away from Devil's tower.

"It's time, gentlemen! The fate of mankind is in our hands! Let's launch that bird!"

Nicola and John quickly started up the diesel powered generators that supplied power to the Chemical Oxygen Iodine Laser and the launch initiator controls. The computer that coordinated the aiming, guidance, and tracking systems had remained booted up since being brought online in the underground powered by a bank of deep cycle marine batteries.

Popeye methodically checked and rechecked the four men's safety equipment. Although they had drilled time and time again, there could be no mistakes. The command booth was designed to protect Carlos by way of its bullet proof glass and air supply system, but this too had not been tested under launch conditions. The rest of the crew would have to take their chances under the truck bed, in specially designed storage boxes that resembled coffins, or at least Popeye thought so. In actuality, the coffins were built to withstand blast pressure and temperatures over three thousand degrees, for upwards to ten minutes, and included an air supply for over two hours. None of them knew for sure if they would survive being that close to the superheated sand storm created by the thrust of the R.A.T.O. motors, but that was the risk a good soldier had to take.

Carlos could see on his monitor that Barry's signal was still slowly gaining altitude and moving away from Devil's Tower, drifting toward the south west well within range. Carlos was torn, this was the only action that he could take and save the world, but what about Barry? Maybe Their ship would soft land and the young man would survive. He knew he could go down in history as either a hero or a monster.

Carlos took a deep breath and then clicked his mouse on the "Launch" icon. Warning lights flashed brightly, a siren screamed, and an automated voice (Nicola had chosen the voice of President Ronald Regan) began the countdown. "Ten," the jet engine on the Bird started winding up; "Nine," the men visually rechecked the power connections; "Eight," they carefully crawled into their coffins and plugged into the air supply system; "Seven," Carlos checked for domestic air traffic. It was all clear; "Six," all four of the Heroes locked down their compartments and body restraints; "Five," Carlos locked in the laser tracking system; "Four," a green "target acquired" message popped up on his monitor; "Three," the laser power generators accelerated to full output; "Two," the docking clamps on the launch tower clanked into the prerelease position; "One," the truck started to vibrate violently as the jet engine spun up to full throttle; "Fire," the two R.A.T.O. engines simultaneously ignited, immediately followed by the detonation of the explosive bolts on the docking clamps. Carlos screamed into the intercom, "Bird's away!!!" The truck nearly bounced off of the ground as the Bird headed skyward, slamming the men around in their compartments much more violently than they had anticipated.

Carlos couldn't see the Bird through the windshield like he had hoped he would. The quarry was completely filled with smoke and strangely glowing dust particles. He had to be content with tracking its progress on his monitor. According to the readouts, the Bird was flying straight and level, slowed to 300 miles per hour, and deployed its wings. A few seconds later, the guidance computer was lining up for a kill shot.

Roy's saucer slowly moved away from its position above Devil's tower; still undetected by Barry or Sergeant Bill's instrument array. The little pilots looked at Roy as if asking his approval for something. Their actions caused Roy to chuckle. The saucer slowed to a stop and began hovering nearly twenty miles to the south west of the Tower. Carlos couldn't believe his eyes. They were just hovering there, like sitting ducks! Suddenly, Barry's signal accelerated to Mach 6, and the Bird accelerated to match Their speed. If they were going to run, they would get a run for their money. The signal from the spacecraft made a smooth arc to the south, and the Bird followed suit.

Nicola, Popeye, and John couldn't handle being locked up in their coffins any longer. Being careful not to unplug their air supply hoses, they climbed out from under the protection of the truck's still glowing heat shielding. The quarry was filled with thick smoke from the R.A.T.O. motors and what they later discovered to be embers from incinerated leaves, floating in the darkness like millions of fireflies.

***

Barry, exhausted from the encounter, collapsed down on his sleeping bag and lay there in near disbelief staring at the night sky. Just before he fell fast asleep, Barry thought he saw something – a star, actually a star shaped diagram. He blinked and rubbed his eyes, but there was nothing else to see. Barry checked his instruments; there was nothing there either. It was time to get some sleep.

***

The Heroes were staring up at the night sky when the laser fired. There was a burst of light, and the ship began darting around the night sky at more than twice the speed of light.

"What happened? Did you guys see that?"

"Carlos. Did we hit the bogy? All I saw was a gigantic star."

"I am absolutely sure it was a direct hit, but I couldn't tell if it had any affect. I just can't tell what happened? All of the systems are fried. Nicola, where is she at?"

"Well.... If the navigation computer is down, then its internal drive is returning the device to its original G.P.S. coordinates, instead of ending up at the bottom of Big Muddy, like it was programmed to do."

"Just what does that mean?"

"Incoming!!!!"

***

Direct hit, sort of

"Hot dog!!! Eight ball in the corner pocket!!!"

The whole family was laughing out loud as the saucer headed into space. It was really nothing at all for the little Visitors to clone Barry's tracking signal device, bring it on board, and fool the Heroes on the ground that were by then running for cover.

***

Otis was on the edge of his seat as the leaders of the world stood with outreached arms, offering a uniquely human symbol of openness, friendship, and trust, awaiting a response from their alien counterparts. Without warning or provocation, the slow moving creatures lunged forward in a synchronized strike, decapitating their hosts. Suddenly, he recoiled in pure horror, and in a subconscious reaction, he scrambled backward up and over the back of his chair; unknowingly letting out a blood curdling scream. Otis fell to the floor in abject unbelief as the screen in front of him blinked into static.

***

The Heroes were still franticly sprinting at top speed away from the launch platform when the ill fated Bird slammed into the floor of the quarry. Luckily for the men, they all reached the pool just before the fireball and debris from the exploding vehicles could overtake them. They all franticly dove as deep into the cold spring water as they could to avoid the red hot shrapnel that was ricocheting off the rock walls of the quarry. From the bottom of the pool, Carlos could see the glow from the flaming pile of junk that used to be the hope for the future of mankind. He couldn't help but wonder if Barry survived the attack. Hopefully, they had achieved their goal of exposing the government cover-ups and proved to the world that we are not alone in the universe. If the sacrifice of a few human lives was required to accomplish that, then so be it.

Minutes later, the soaked and dejected men crawled out of the water and collapsed on the cold rock floor of the quarry.

"That was interesting. Hey, Carlos, where do you think they went down?"

"Hopefully, somewhere that the public can find the wreckage before the military has a chance to cover it up again, if it went down at all."

"How are we going to confirm anything without the scanners?"

"The old fashioned way; I will make a phone call and ask. Meanwhile, we need to get out of this hole in the ground and fast, before we get swarmed by forest rangers and tree huggers."

Carlos was trying to keep the mood light, but they all knew that authorities would have too many questions if they were caught. The forest road that led to the highway wound around the base of mountain and would be the first place that the authorities would look so the fugitives headed straight up to the planned extraction point on a high glade opening in the pitch blackness. Popeye took the lead, following a G.P.S. unit that he always kept in his possibles bag, Nicola and John followed close behind.

"Go on ahead while I make that phone call, men. I will catch up."

"Order some pizza while you're at it! I'm starving! Make one double cheese! Ha!"

After an exhausting climb to the summit, the men collapsed into the thick grass and waited for daybreak, which by that time was less than an hour away.

Carlos waited until the other men were out of earshot before keying in the number on his security encrypted satellite phone. The device would be nearly impossible to hold and dial at the same time for a person with only one hand, but fortunately for Carlos, he had access to the most preeminent technology available. The robotic hand would never be as good as a real one, but he had high hopes that someday medical science would catch up. Maybe now it would.

"Good morning, Brother. Are you and Barry enjoying your trip to Devil's Tower?"

Carlos could tell by the tone of his half brother's voice that their mission had been an utter failure. He was very disappointed but, on some level, he was relieved that Barry was unharmed.

***

Plausible Deniability

Barry awoke at dawn, yawned, and rubbed the sleep from his eyes. The sun was peeking over the eastern edge of the football field sized plateau at the top of Devil's Tower. A pair of chipmunks scurried around among the mesquite bushes and cactus that made up most of the sparse ground cover. Barry was always amazed at nature, its weaknesses and its strengths. Just to think about how the plants got to the top of that great monolith was one thing, seeds carried by the wind or birds, but the chipmunks. How on Earth did they get up there?

As he gathered his equipment and prepared to repel down the treacherous tower slope, he contemplated whether the events of last night were a dream or not. The survival training that he had received from Sergeant Bill also included highly honed tracking abilities. Barry had once tracked a running deer in the dark, up a mountain, in a blizzard, with nothing but a cigarette lighter, or at least that is what he liked to tell Sergeant Bill when he wanted him to find his glasses or the TV remote.

Barry stood there in total amazement; there were several sets of foot prints surrounding his camp site. Most of tracks were made by the hundreds of climbers that frequent the Tower every year, but on top of the climbing boot tracks were three sets of other prints. A huge smile spread across his face. He knew that he hadn't been dreaming. Imprinted ever so slightly in the gravely ground, there was one set of prints, human sized, with what seemed to be some kind of deck shoe sole print and two sets of oddly shaped child sized prints that had no sole marks at all. The best part, none of the prints came from anywhere or went anywhere. He hadn't been dreaming! Barry stifled the temptation to jump and yell for joy because he knew that Sergeant Bill would be watching.

It took Barry nearly 90 minutes to descend from the summit and make his way to the camp ground. As he approached the armored recreational vehicle that he temporarily called home, Sergeant Bill met him at the door.

"Good morning, Barry. Did you see any of those little green men?"

"Nope, Sergeant. Didn't see nuthin but stars."

"Well, better luck next time. Are you hungry? I just about have breakfast ready."

"Yes, Sir!!! I could eat the butt off of a road killed Yak!!"

"Then, you're in luck!! Found one in the parking lot!! Got a call this morning early, about an hour before you started your descent."

"Ahh! What is Uncle Wayne up to besides not looking at his watch?"

"He said that he was Elk hunting in the Northern Rockies near the Canadian border, would be gone a couple of more weeks."

"Well, good for him. He deserves a vacation. Honestly, I don't know how Uncle Wayne does it. The boredom would do me in. I know that he keeps his thumb on the grunts at 51 even when he's not physically there. So is there anything exciting going on?

"Nothing much, other than a couple of routine satellite flyovers, some tourists getting too close, and, get this, that photographer was back on the peak again watching the base. Security sent a Raptor and an Apache, and he didn't even blink."

"I don't think old Sam is any real threat any way. What do you think, Sergeant?"

"He might be, under the right circumstances, but his worth as plausible deniability cover far outweighs the risk. Without the kooks that he keeps stirred up, some of the most secret testing couldn't go on. As you know, the best way to hide something classified is in plain sight. If they think what they see is a flying saucer piloted by little green men, rather than what it really is, then so be it. Like the old saying; "What they don't know won't hurt em.""

"Sometimes he is hard to read, and I know that we have to trust him with our lives, but are you sure that there isn't anything else going on?"

"Barry, if there is anyone on this Earth that you can trust it's your Uncle Wayne."

***

Otis sat there sobbing in unbelief, staring at the blank blue screen. What would he do now? What could he do? What would the world do? He was still inconsolable when his private nurse rushed into the room.

"Mister Otis, come on and let me put you into bed. I know that you really love watching television all night, but enough is enough!"

"But! But! You don't understand!"

"Don't worry, Mister Otis. The satellite must have blown down in the storm. I will make sure to rent that movie for you so you can see the end."

"Promise?"

"I promise!"

***

There's good news and there's bad news!

The sun was rising over the low desert hills surrounding Peek-a-boo Peak when Sam Drocer awoke in his camping chair. He had spent another fruitless night in search of something that he still believed deep in his gut did exist. Although this excursion into the unknown was a complete waste of time, he knew that he was not about to give up.

Sam checked each piece of his equipment as he put it away in his backpack. He was hoping that the automatic tracking system of some of the instruments might have caught something more than meteors or man-made aircraft in the night sky as he slept. Two of his long-range cameras had captured the images of a military jet and some sort of helicopter but nothing else.

As he made his way down the path to his beat up old Blazer, he started contemplating his life. Sam was tired of living alone. Could he still have the American dream or was he too old to start now? Then he remembered the tumor growing in his head. Why had he forgotten the tumor? It had been on his mind constantly since his diagnosis last summer.

As Sam arrived at his blazer, he realized that he wasn't exhausted like he usually was after the six mile ride on the old Trailbreaker. Amazingly, he wasn't even tired. Actually, he hadn't felt this good in years.

Sam loaded the bike on to the trailer, stowed his equipment, and then jumped into the driver's seat for the long drive home. Slowly moving along the bumpy trail, as usual, he checked his mirrors. He was startled when he caught a glimpse of his own face in the mirror and drove over a mesquite bush, nearly high centering the blazer. He couldn't believe his eyes. What Sam was looking at was an image of himself from 20 years ago.

Sam somehow knew deep in his psyche that it was some kind of a gift, payment for something, but he couldn't even begin to guess what.

The old blazer rumbled down the desert back road that eventually led to the extraterrestrial highway, leaving a dust trail a mile long. Bumping and jolting along through the ruts, potholes, and the occasional dry creek bed, Sam still couldn't believe how good he felt. He had stopped a couple of times along the way to check the mirror and still couldn't believe how he looked. What had happened to him? Was he sent back in time? Sam checked the date and time on his cell phone; no service as usual, but the date and time were correct. Was it some kind of government experiment? Was it some kind of metaphysical convergence or a miracle of God? At that point, Sam didn't really care. He felt like he could take on the world. He hadn't felt this good since he was a young pup.

Sam was nearly to the turn off that would take him back to the highway when he noticed a Jeep sitting among the sagebrush, about 300 yards off of the beaten path. Coming to a stop, he pulled his pair of binoculars from the storage compartment in the console of the old Blazer and began searching the area. Usually, he paid no attention to the odd vehicle that wandered into the wasteland surrounding the mountains, but for some reason his curiosity got the better of him.

There were a lot of things to consider when approaching any abandoned vehicle: it could be a trap of some kind, it could be drug runners, it could be a crime scene, and a person never knows what kind of a jam they could get themselves into.

After about ten minutes of probing the surrounding wilderness, Sam started to drive on. After driving a short distance up the road, he decided to stop and look again. He didn't really know why, there was just something, a feeling, a tug at his inner being. Sam raised the binoculars to his eyes again and meticulously scanned the topography. Just as he was about to give up again, he spotted something odd protruding out from under a large bush about 200 yards away from the abandoned Jeep, up on the crest of a small hill.

A chill went up Sam's spine; it was a pair of legs. Sam pulled and checked the .45 auto that he kept on his hip for snakes and other dangerous critters and then laid it on the passenger seat. Against his better judgment, he cautiously turned around and drove over to the Jeep. Slowly slipping out of the truck's seat, Sam began painstakingly investigating the scene. No one was there, and there didn't seem to be anything out of the ordinary except for the fact that this Jeep was so far off the road. The top was up, but the doors were unlocked. There was a pile of women's clothes piled in the back floorboard, a cooler with ice and sport drinks in the rear, and a large aluminum case in the front passenger seat. If it wasn't for the motionless legs that he had spotted earlier, Sam would have driven away. Whoever that was on the hilltop was definitely in some kind of trouble and he was the only one that could help.

With gun in hand and the safety off, Sam stealthily trudged through the brush and rocks up the slope toward the body in the brush, carefully scrutinizing his every step. He had to stay focused on where he was. A rattle snake or scorpion bite was the last thing he needed. There were so many unseen dangers out there; an inexperienced hiker could die before help could come. Most of the deaths in the region were caused by the party getting lost and then dying from heat stroke. Many of them were less than a mile from safety.

Sam stopped in his tracks as he slowly stepped around the opposite side of the bush where the body was laying. The body appeared to belong to a person that knew what they were doing. High top boots to protect from snake bite, heavy denim pants with a leather bottom for sliding down over rocks, a light tan shirt to reflect the heat of the summer sun. Sam was thinking, "What kind of mistake did this guy make?" Fearing the worst, he quietly knelt down and gently nudged one of the feet with the muzzle of his pistol. Almost immediately, Sam found himself looking down the bore of the biggest revolver he had ever seen. He remained crouching in place, frozen in complete astonishment.

"Sam!!! What are you doing out here?"

Sam fell to his back with sudden relief. Nearly simultaneously, Susann jumped to her feet and stood over him with a wildly puzzled look on her face.

"That is you, isn't it? You look so young! I get it; you have to be Sam's son!!!!!"

"No Susann, it's me!!!!! It's me!!!!! I don't know what has happened to me either!!!!! I woke up this morning, and I was like this. I feel like I'm twenty years younger, and I think that the cancer is gone!!!!!!"

"Cancer???? Is that why??? We have a lot to talk about, Mister Sam Drocer!!!"

"Yes, we do, starting with what are you doing out here, and where did you get that hog leg you are carrying?"

"Oh, this little thing? It's called a "Hip Cannon." My dad made it for me when I first started coming out here. I carry it for snakes and other wildlife that might sneak up on me while I am sneaking up on other things. That didn't make any sense to me. Did it to you? Anyway, it will shoot twenty gauge shotgun shells and even flairs. He insisted that I have some sort of defense. I guess it is a dad thing. He was afraid that someone would carry me off or something. Pretty lucky I had it with me, right? Wow, I am talking a mile a minute! What are you doing out here?"

"Oh man, it's a camera case! I didn't even think about that possibility when I saw you laying up here in the bushes. I thought that someone was dead, and I almost was. Man, you are really fast with that thing."

"Just one more thing that you don't know about me!!!"

"Well, I would like to try and make up time figuring out the rest of your little secrets. Are you hungry? I know a little diner not too far from here that serves the best hamburgers in Nevada!"

As Sam and Susann made their way back down to the desert floor, they couldn't keep their eyes off of each other. Sam was thinking to himself how the miracle that had come over him was going to change everything. Maybe he could have a life with Susann!!!

Suddenly a familiar sound caught their attention. Sam reached for his pistol and quickly looked around for the rattlesnake. Susann saw that the six feet long sidewinder was not within striking range, took her hand off of the hip cannon, gave out a calculated scream, and jumped into Sam's arms. Looking deeply into each other's eyes, they finally shared their first kiss.

***

The Journey Begins

The saucer slipped silently out of Earth's atmosphere and accelerated effortlessly to a quite leisurely pace of two times the speed of light. The route was chosen by the Navigators so that the Smiths could get a good look at all of the planets in their solar system. From their pods, they could see the moon, and then Mars, in great detail while in actuality they were flying by like light poles at the side of the interstate. Slowing down and going back to the dark side of Jupiter to avoid being spotted by the telescopes of Earth, they could see the Mothership that they knew from their implanted memories. The Smith family shuttle and the other small ships navigated gracefully in through a vast gaping opening on the bottom of the gigantic space cruiser. The hole looked as though the interior of the ship was open to space, but they knew from their implanted memories that the portal (large enough to tow a cruise ship through) was actually protected by a very robust force field. After triumphantly circling the interior of the cavernous ship, the shuttle came to rest on communal mezzanine near the garden.

"I'm sorry that we haven't had the time to sit and talk. There will be time soon, I promise! Right now, our hosts want to meet my family."

Stepping out of their pods, the family couldn't help but stand and stare at each other. The change in each of them was dramatic. Brad, Toby and Sylvia appeared to be the same age, about twenty Earth years. The most exciting of the transformations was in their mother and father. Roy and Ronnie had been returned to the age that they were when they had last been together almost 30 years ago. Roy couldn't take his eyes off of his young wife. Her hair had returned to its glorious blond luster and was once again hanging nearly to her waist. Her care worn face now had the look of health and energy. Ronnie turned and smiled at Roy, her hazel eyes twinkling with excitement.

"Does this mean we will live forever, Roy?"

"No, Ronnie, only God can do that, but we will live a long, long time, much longer than on Earth. That is one of the reasons why they had to bring me back. You were at the brink of death, and I couldn't let that happen."

Roy was beyond ecstatic that she was safe, that his whole family was safe.

The great ship was silent as Roy and his family walked out to the inner edge of the immense concourse located directly in front of their saucer shaped craft. As suddenly as the memories had been implanted into their minds at the desert air base, there came a new flood of information.

Immediately they knew the names and faces of every being aboard the ship (including the "others"- humans) and all of the little Friends knew them as well. The human introductions would have to wait until later. Roy turned to his reunited family and asked them a question.

"They want to know if they can speak with you. Can they have your permission?"

The overwhelming consensus was a resounding "yes" and, with their newly acquired psychic connection, they could hear the greetings of the multitude in residence aboard the Mothership. The other humans had also gathered on the concourse to welcome Roy's family onboard, but, unnoticed by Roy, one was missing.

Ronnie turned and kissed Roy, and the crowd went wild. Suddenly, tens of thousands of the little grayish silver beings leaped into the seemingly empty central chamber flipping and flopping very joyously in the zero gravity zone. The whole group of humans was dumbfounded at the outrageous new behavior. When they thought they had seen it all, the odd celebration display became even odder. Three brightly glowing, orange globes approximately twenty feet in diameter floated gently into the swarm of writhing bodies bouncing them in all directions.

The scene looked like a combination of beach ball and billiards. The little creatures bounced off the globes, the walls, and each other. At first, even Roy didn't know what to make of the spectacle, until he heard the hilarious infectious psychic laughter. He had no idea that the little beings could be that funny. Unable to keep from joining in, Roy and the entire Smith family (Roy decided to become a Smith himself) were soon belly laughing also. It was the most that he had laughed for over 30 years Everyone was still trying to regain their composure and wipe the tears of laughter from their eyes when they discovered that the central chamber was empty again and totally dark. Deep in the blackness, there could be seen a swarm of tiny lights. As the lights grew brighter, the onlookers could tell that it was an armada of small shuttle ships. Each craft was pulsating with a myriad of very bright multicolored lights and darting around in the darkness forming one beautiful pattern and then another. After several minutes of being amazed by the armada's display, a lone unlit ship made its approach toward the enthralled crowd of spectators. The light from the concourse illuminated the darkened ship as it drew close enough for Sylvia and Toby to recognize it.

Sylvia laughed and exclaimed, "Hey look! It's the flying pickle!"

All of the humans burst into laughter. After regaining his composure, Roy was still giggling.

"It does look like a pickle!!"

With the addition of the psychic connection, the little Friends finally understood the analogy and began chirping loudly in approval of the humor. After several minutes of chirping and laughter, the welcome display began again. The Flying Pickle moved back into the darkness as the other small ships retreated to form a model of Earth's solar system minus the Sun. As the "planets and moon" began their rotation, the Pickle took up station in the center of the diagram and started its presentation. Brilliant multicolored lights began pulsating from the "blisters" on its hull, followed by a mind-boggling laser light display that lit up the entire interior of the Mothership. Just when the Smiths thought they had seen it all, the Pickle lowered its lights and formed a spherical cloud obscuring it from view.

Inside the cloud cover that was held in place by a force field, the Pickle slowly turned on its lights and began rotating end over end. With each revolution, the Pilots would vary the axis of the spin slightly. As the revolutions increased in velocity so did the intensity of the lights. Faster, brighter, faster, brighter, until the cloud in the middle of the solar system diagram was a continuous ultra bright orb of light rivaling Earth's star for its beauty. The Pickle had redeemed itself.

The small crowd of silent spectators was so mesmerized by the prowess and expertise of the exhibition that they didn't notice the rumbling sound approaching them from the airspace above them. Brad was the first to recognize it - the cadence of a V-12 Rolls Royce engine with its superchargers screaming. No sooner had he spotted the World War II P51 Mustang, than the old war bird dove toward the crowd and fired all six of its fifty caliber machine guns. The whole group of humans dove to the deck of the platform instinctively while the nonhumans stood and chirped loudly in approval. As they scrambled to their feet, the Mustang made another pass. This time, it did a barrel roll close enough to feel the majestic aircraft's prop wash and to see the pilot's laughing face. Realizing that the engine noise and machine gun fire was just a sound effect, Roy stepped to the edge of the platform and yelled.

"I hate you, Mary Smith!"

Roy began laughing loudly as the P51 landed and began taxiing toward them. After he caught his composure, Roy started telling about his love-hate relationship with "that crazy Wasp" when something clicked in Brad's mind. Sylvia noticed the astonished look on his face.

"What's up, big brother? You look like you've seen a ghost."

***

The Mothership slowly pulled away from its hiding place behind Jupiter, being careful not to disturb the high gravity atmosphere, preventing the formation of another big red spot on the surface. Although it was very doubtful that any Earthlings could even remotely track the path of the gigantic interstellar flying city, the Navigators weren't taking any chances. Quickly accelerating to near top speed with a velocity far too great to be tracked by any humanly devised instrument, leaving Earth's home planetary system behind, they were on their way! The Mothership took the "scenic tour" to well beyond the Milky Way, then circled back around, going down and under Earth's solar system in a counter rotating path around and behind the Sun.

The now complete family that had been pulled apart all those years ago was too busy building and rebuilding their lives to take any notice of where the great ship was heading. Despite the ordeal of the last couple of days and the anticipation of coming events, they were all exhausted but very glad to finally be all together. Wherever home was going to be didn't matter because, after all, home is where the heart is.

Once again the immense flying city slowed to a leisurely three thousand miles an hour as it entered the gravitational field of Homeworld. All of the Earthlings and thousands of the "little ones" gathered around the huge viewing ports on the common observation concourse as their home for the last 35 years slowly glided between the two silvery moons that were orbiting the most beautiful planet in the universe. This time the Mothership did not hide but triumphantly turned on all of her lights and audio arrays and launched most of the small ships in a spectacular display that could rival the Sun itself for beauty. From a huge three dimensional display floating in the middle of the cavernous ship, all of the ship's occupants could see and hear their arrival as if they were on the planet looking up into the night sky.

Although the little ones communicated telepathically, the Earthlings could feel their joy, and the chirping sound that they did make was almost deafening. Turning their attention back to the external viewing ports, the ship slowly swung around to the daylight side of the shimmering greenish blue orb. The sight was nearly overwhelming to all of the observers. Hanging in space before them was a planet roughly the same size as Earth but vastly different in almost every other way. There were no polar caps, no rain, no snow, and no seasonal changes. This world had no axis wobble that would let solar dust into the atmosphere at the poles.

No land masses or oceans were observable from space because of the green house-like water vapor barrier surrounding the entire planet, causing the atmospheric pressure to be approximately twice that of Earth, allowing the flora and fauna to thrive. Homeworld was literally a tropical paradise.

As it turns out, in part, Sergeant Bill and many others on Earth were right. The Extraterrestrials were hiding something, one of the biggest secrets in the universe, not for conquest or domination but for their own protection. This was one of those secrets that may never be able to be told on Earth.

The Beginning

CPSIA information can be obtained
at www.ICGtesting.com
Printed in the USA
BVHW082145030620
580887BV00015B/492